a Slim Green Silence

Beverly Rycroft

UMUZI

Published in 2015 by Umuzi
an imprint of Penguin Random House (Pty) Ltd
Company Reg No 1953/000441/07
Estuaries No 4, Oxbow Crescent, Century Avenue,
Century City, 7441, South Africa
PO Box 1144, Cape Town, 8000, South Africa
umuzi@randomstruik.co.za
www.randomstruik.co.za

First edition, first printing 2015
1 3 5 7 9 8 6 4 2

ISBN 978-1-4152-0738-3 (Print)
ISBN 978-1-4152-0626-3 (ePub)
ISBN 978-1-4152-0627-0 (PDF)

Cover design and illustration by Gretchen van der Byl
Author photograph by Ben Rycroft
Text design by Chérie Collins
Set in 10.5 on 14.5 pt Janson

Printed and bound by Paarl Media,
Jan van Riebeeck Avenue, Paarl, South Africa

For my mother,
Una Scheepers

The quality of mercy is not strain'd,
It droppeth as the gentle rain from heaven
Upon the place beneath.

– WILLIAM SHAKESPEARE, *The Merchant of Venice*

Chapter 1

WITH THE DAWN LIGHT starting to pool around the houses in the Scheepersdorp Valley, all the changes have begun floating to the surface. I'm looking particularly at the outside of number twenty-two Plumbago Way: the peeling paint on the walls and the tiny, greasy fingerprints on the brass handle of my front door. How long has it been? Six months? A year?

The house looks smaller from this height, as if it's squatting under the sky like a toadstool. The back yard and the plot behind it are laid out like a drawing, the perimeter fence a thick pencil line.

Below this cluster of roofs are all the people I ever loved.

Right here, next to the front steps, is where I sowed a bunch of vygies in the shape of an M. That was in my last autumn. I'd half hoped to be here to see them come up myself. If not, I still liked the idea of it dawning slowly on Bart or my sister Sylvia what I'd done. Though even now, I can't tell you how Bart fitted in with me. Lover? Friend? A bit of both, I suppose.

At the time, I'd pictured him stumbling across my planted message, stopping to wipe a tear – till somebody happened to notice him. Or giving a grim smile. I never was quite sure if Bart enjoyed my jokes or found them too dark at times.

None of that matters now. At least not to me, or the me I find myself to be. I'm no longer a set of organs neatly packed and stitched inside a skin. More like an orbiting planet. A consciousness.

Driven by what? Revenge? Curiosity? Irritation?

Because I *can* see the front lawn needs mowing. And the flower beds are riddled with watergrass.

There was a stage when seeing that mess would have set me off big time. I'd have been desperate to get stuck in and make it all neat and right again.

Not any more. That urge to weed and feed and prune dissolved long ago. The only thing pulling me on now is the *thud, thud, thud* of footsteps down the wooden passage of my house.

Keeping pace, I flit past the windows. I peer in at the framed photos on the walls, and notice they're thick with dust. Apart from that, not much has changed: the faded striped wallpaper, the worn runners on the passage floor, the doors opening onto chaotic bedrooms. Sylvia, Marianne, Bart. So far, so pretty much the same. Except for one large photo at the end. Even from outside, it's not hard to recognise the sturdy figure pictured there. She's wearing shorts and a halter-top that shows a cleavage everyone knew she secretly treasured. That thick, coarse hair. It would have been a darker blonde if it hadn't been bleached so often by the sun. Straight as straw, no matter how it got cut, so it was either braided into a thick plait or pulled back in a pony, like in the photo. A roughly cut fringe that's not quite grown out, sticking up in places. And on her tanned face the scowl I practised in the mirror each day.

Someone with a sense of humour put that picture up. One veldskoened foot, knee raised, is planted on a heap of branches and leaves. In the opposite hand she's holding a pitchfork. All that's needed to complete the picture is an arrow-tipped tail twining out from that ample, denimed rump. Very funny, Bart.

Though a kinder person might say he chose that photo for the crinkle round my mocking brown eyes, the pinch of nostrils and lips that suggest I, too, am just about to laugh.

On towards the kitchen the skinny figure thumps, with a solid little shape perched, swaying, on her hip. And she's still humming that annoying tune. Princess. All the way down the passage it nags at me, until her bare feet stomp onto the kitchen tiles and she swings the child to the floor.

I don't care to look too closely. At the kitchen. At the child. I can see enough to tell what a disgrace the place has become. Dirty dishes cluttering the sink. Plastic building blocks piled up in the corner. I'd rather stay outside, peering through the kitchen window. Not quite in, not quite out.

Story of my life, some might say.

The kettle plumes steam, and my fox terrier Jakkals shakes herself awake from her basket in the corner, neck hairs rising. She trots towards the window and starts to bark.

"Quiet, Jakkals!" someone shouts. A lanky figure is lounging with his back to the kitchen sink. "Lekker day, hey?" he says to Princess, and turns to look out of the window.

He could be staring straight at me.

His brown hair's still spiked in front, but it's growing out some tacky blond highlights, and behind it's grown right down to his collar. *Business in front, party at the back*, he'd described it once.

By the look of him, I'd guess he must be just short of his thirtieth birthday now, though he's been trying to hide those grey hairs since he was twenty-six. A ray of sun glances through the window, forming a halo over his scraggy fringe.

No question about it. I'm stirred by the pink colour in those acne-scarred cheeks. The glow in those bottle-green eyes. The gangly arms and wrists emerging from the sleeves of his white tee-shirt, twitching like they're itching to get to work.

As if.

Still, if I *could* remember how it felt to be happy, it would be now. Because there's not a hint of a shadow under my old friend Alwyn van der Walt's eyes. Not a tremor or wobble to betray him. In and out his breath slides from his lungs, like silk. As if he doesn't need to think about it any more.

If I could, I might even be tempted to grab his hands, waltz him round my kitchen and shout so loudly his mother could hear from next door.

See? It's true. Life *does* goes on.

As if to prove it, Princess pushes Alwyn rudely aside and plunges a saucepan into the sink. Despite her pint-sized frame, she manages to shift him without any trouble. "Today," her voice booms, "we gonna do this other thing." Princess swirls the pot under the tap. "I have the dream last night that today is the right day for this."

This is not the voice that would ask me tentatively for another loan or the afternoon off. It's not the high, diffident voice that once used to answer my phone: *Hullo good day is Princess speaking how can I help you?* This voice is gravelly and hoarse. This is the voice of a Boss.

"I going to clean the kitchen now," – Princess slams the pot on the drainer – "then I going to give Marianne the porridge. Then your mother she going to take her for me." She wrenches the plug from the sink and the water gurgles into the gutter outside. "*Then* we going down there," she says in her Boss voice. "Half past eleven. You must meet me there by that place half past eleven."

Somewhere on the edge of Alwyn's consciousness he's taking in everything Princess is telling him. But anyone who knows him well enough can tell that another thought is barging through, shifting Princess's words to one side.

"I dreamed about Connie last night," says Alwyn at last. He nods at the window, as if he really *does* see me drifting in front of him. "She was down there, down by the river. She swung over on the rope, then she was standing there on the bank by Papendorf's old place, calling me to come over." He leans his bony wrists on the windowsill to push his face forward and stare out at the land behind my house; so close I can see needle-flecks of yellow and green in his eyes, as if they're reflecting the leaves of the yellow-wood tree.

Which, I've already made sure, is still growing untouched in the middle of the plot.

In fact, it's clear nobody's touched anything. The plumbago at the back fence is at least ten centimetres higher, and so are the shrubs dipping into the river. But the Port Jackson saplings have seeded on the side of the plot adjoining my neighbour Harry Healey's property, and a lantana has taken hold on the river bank, almost strangling a thorn tree. I'm surprised Harry hasn't yet climbed in to do a slash and burn. Particularly now I'm no longer around to stop him.

Still, the rest seems as it should be. The river at the bottom of the plot is swollen with spring rain, and white-eyes are picking away at the plumbago. Underneath the tickling birds, the shrub stands passive as a cow. In and out of the glass surface of the kitchen window the two images recede and surge, the birds on the plumbago and Alwyn's earnest face.

Chapter 2

THE FIRST TIME I suspected there might be something genuinely wrong with Alwyn van der Walt was that winter's day we climbed the Kanonkop together, about a year and a half before Marianne was born.

The two of us grew up next door to each other in houses parked at the foot of the Kop in the Scheepersdorp Valley. Alwyn was only nine months older than me, and we'd played together literally from the moment I could sit, when our mothers would plonk us on a blanket in our back yard. Nobody knew that mountain better than we did.

At seven, we learned to climb over the Healeys' fence. We never looked back. After that, Alwyn and I knew all we had to do was nip through Harry's back yard and down the side of his house to find the path to the Kop. Most days after school that's what we did, Sylvia sometimes tagging along, though she was two years younger and usually dropped out halfway.

Climbing the Kop was never a big deal to Alwyn and me. But I did notice, that day, how he kept stopping to rest, and how loud his breathing was. I didn't want to encourage him. For a twenty-six-year-old man, he had a lot on his plate. The month before, he'd diagnosed himself with pneumonia, though the doctor called it flu. Three months before it had been pleurisy, and the month before that, foot-and-mouth disease.

So when I heard him breathing like that, and saw him bending over to rest his hands on his knees, I carried on without saying anything. We'd been arguing all the way up, as usual, so I thought he was just looking for an excuse. We were fighting about where we'd seen the paintbrush lilies last year. Every spring we staked out the places where we found bulbs, marking a rock or a tree so we could come back in winter. If there were enough by then, we took a half-dozen home to plant in the plot of wild land that stretched down to the river behind both our houses.

"Here." We were only halfway up the Kop, but I stopped at a clearing I'd made sure to remember. I knew I'd seen the lilies growing there last spring, just left of a big clump of aloes. I'd carried a backpack up with a bottle of water and a trowel, leaving Alwyn to struggle manfully with a Checkers bag for the bulbs.

"What's the matter?" I asked eventually. I was sniffling around trying to find the marker I'd made for the lilies. "You hung over again?"

"No way," Alwyn panted, "I went to bed early last night."

"You're bloody unfit."

At last I found the rock with the cross I'd painted in Sylvia's red nail polish. I knelt beside it and started to dig.

"You need to start exercising again. And eating properly."

"Ja, I don't know, Con, I don't think it's that, hey."

Alwyn lay back against a flat-sided rock, stretching out his long legs and folding his arms behind his head. "I think maybe I got diabetes. Or multiple cirrhosis."

"Who've you been listening to now? *You* magazine?"

"No, now," – holding up his index finger – "I know you won't believe me, Con, but you must listen, hey. I was talking to a oke the other day who said, after a bad bout of flu, you can do a real damage to your heart."

"Only if you exert yourself."

"And this oke, he said to me, he said: Alwyn. Man. You must take it easy."

"I am happy to see," I panted as I dug away at the hard soil, "his words did not fall on deaf ears."

I dropped the trowel and felt the bulbs nudge into my hands. There were at least twenty, but I only wanted a half-dozen for the plot. One by one I delivered them from the ground: six scarred, pink secrets. I held them up and turned to Alwyn, grinning. I couldn't believe it when I saw he was fast asleep.

We were unlikely friends, Alwyn and I. But then there's not a huge selection pool in a small town like Scheepersdorp. I'm saying this from his point of view as well as mine.

One of the things I liked most about him was he never took it personally when I didn't feel like company. When I locked myself in a room with a pile of books from the Scheepersdorp Library, he went fishing or tinkered with one of the cars parked in his mother's yard. I didn't care about those things, and Alwyn never opened a book unless it had a picture of a motorbike or a fish on the cover.

Alwyn liked to pretend he worked for a living, but there wasn't any need. He earned some money doing odd jobs around Scheepersdorp, but his mom had a paid-off house and a generous pension from her late husband. It made her happy to see her only child rested and well fed. And Alwyn liked making his mother happy.

When things got so bad with him that he couldn't get out of

bed, I used to go next door and read to him. I read him articles from *Car* magazine, and of course from the latest issue of *Tight Lines*. But also a few stories, sometimes even a poem. Langston Hughes' "Mother to Son", for example. He asked me to read that to him twice.

I wasn't in the best shape myself by then, so we must have made a sorry pair. I guess neither of us liked thinking too much about the days we climbed the Kanonkop for bulbs. Though I was never really sure if he used to come along because he enjoyed the walk, or because we were friends and he liked being with me.

Chapter 3

THE BIG HAND ON THE clock above the kitchen stove is on twelve, and the small hand's about to hit six. I know it's morning. And I'm pretty sure it's November. For starters, the nasturtiums at the kitchen door are blooming. The plot behind the house is a dozen shades of green, and thick with stalks and buds. Also: the Scheepersdorp Butchery calendar Prestiked to the fridge is set to November. Sylvia was always unusually picky about drawing, each morning, a thick line through the previous day. She liked marking people's birthdays and anniversaries, so she could be sure to phone or take over a bunch of wild flowers or some homemade rusks.

Today there's a red ring drawn around 4th November. Some-one – I recognise Sylvia's hand – has written *Connie* outside the red circle, though I know for certain my birthday was 18th April. And that I died before I could turn twenty-nine.

It was a day like this. I remember that, too. Early summer, sunny and green.

Could it be a year since I died?

And if I'm right … why am I home again?

The minute I start wondering that, I'm contracted back into

the air. Within a millisecond, I'm so far away that the kitchen window of number twenty-two is the size of a fish scale, and the whole of Scheepersdorp lies below me.

On the face of it, it seems like just another summer morning in the valley. The dawn light's silvering the seams of houses and windows. Dogs and roosters are beginning to stir, and the occasional back door opens and claps shut again.

It *is* rather odd that Harry Healey's not up and about yet. By now, he should be pumping the accelerator on his Nissan bakkie, trying to swear it into starting up. Or pacing around his orchard, checking for ripe fruit. But the bakkie's parked in his front driveway, and even Harry's dogs aren't barking yet.

The other strange sight is the Boatman climbing the Kanonkop. He's clearly had no trouble finding the path that starts at Harry Healey's side fence, and he's already halfway up to the plateau. It's not difficult to recognise him. You don't get too many men with Afros and Carducci suits going up there.

When he reaches the plateau, the Boatman squats below the red rock. He shades his eyes to pan his gaze across the valley, hand and face dark against the dazzling white cuff of his shirt. He's in the exact same spot where Alwyn and I used to hide and spy on everyone in town. For a moment I wonder if he's looking for me.

"Any idea why you're back?" he asked earlier. I still can't think of a reply. Though I'm pretty sure he knows more about the situation than I do.

Neither of us said a word on the way over. For me, it was all too sudden: the warped bench of the boat, the oars slicing into the water, the light creeping towards us from above the Kanonkop in a thin, crooked line. And the man opposite me dressed in white shirt and tails, as if he were about to attend a wedding.

We must have rowed in silence for about half an hour before

he pushed the boat gently to shore. He sat back and rested his hands on the oars, one over the other. They were strangely tiny compared to the rest of him, and the pearly nails gleamed against his mahogany fingers. I tried working out how tall he was: close on six foot, and broad, with a healthy paunch lapping over his belt. Genuine leather, if I'm not mistaken. What fascinated me most was the pink scar running up his left wrist and disappearing into the cuff of his starched white shirt.

I could feel him watching me as I headed off along the shore of the dam towards Scheepersdorp in the dawn light. My hair lay in a thick plait down my back, and I wore a blouse and a faded cotton skirt that whipped smartly in the breeze. In some strange way, I was beginning to remember how people managed to push themselves off, heel-toe, heel-toe, to move their legs forward and walk.

If there's one thing you can count on in Scheepersdorp, it's this: at six-thirty each morning a jagged scream is going to pelt out from behind the Kanonkop. Almost immediately, the sky will cloud over and a rippling orange-green carpet of parrots will tear through the valley to drop to the plot below. Exactly fifteen seconds later, the back door at Harry Healey's place will rip open and a gun will go off. On a good day, it will be a pellet gun or a .22. On bad days, only the shotgun will do.

If you're going to live here, you're just going to have to get used to it, I heard Harry tell a newcomer once. And most people have. Some locals still come out onto their stoeps in pyjamas and dressing gown each morning to check out Harry's aim, but the rest just put their pillows over their ears and tell themselves it never lasts too long.

The hand on the kitchen clock at my old house is chopping off the seconds towards six-thirty. The sun is edging up into the blue sky above the Kanonkop. From the plateau on the Kop the Boatman looks up, straight at me. It feels like the town is holding its breath. One, two, three …

A rock dove flutters across to perch on one of the pecan-nut trees behind Harry's back door. Down on the plot, the branches of the yellowwood tree tremble in the breeze.

In the puzzling silence I can hear the calm rhythm of Princess's blood pushing in and out, and Alwyn's heart pounding away in his chest, miraculously steady. And – what I've been avoiding all along – the fresh, quick pulse of the small heart I once heard from the monitor of an ultrasound.

I draw nearer again. Sunlight is streaming in through the kitchen window, over the unwashed pots and plates in the kitchen sink, shading them from grey to yellow to gold. A crumbed bread board, sticky spoons, the steaming pot of porridge. The light collects in the corner of the kitchen, fuzzing a crown of blonde hair. A teeny fist lifts a wooden spoon and bangs it on an overturned saucepan.

There's something of my sister Sylvia in that wide forehead. Though you can hardly see it through the blonde fringe falling over her eyes. She's got Sylvia's hair, too, even though Sylvia is a brunette. The thick, kinked bush that Sylvia once blow-dried tame every morning is growing the way God decreed on this tiny head.

The child gets to her feet. Except for a sagging nappy, she's wearing only a sleeveless white vest, spotted with porridge. She waddles across the kitchen to pull at Princess's skirt. The way she totters eagerly forward, though she's barely learned to walk, confident of an open-armed welcome. The cheerful pump of the arms. She doesn't get that from me.

But the way she turns her fat cheek and angles her head to look up at Princess. Her blue glare and the way she holds her head on one side, thinking. The sheer determination in that pose.

That's all mine.

I chose the name Marianne from *Sense and Sensibility*. I wanted the child to have some spirit and not be too much of a good girl. Mostly because, the very first time I clapped eyes on her, I saw how much she looked like Sylvia.

Sylvia's more like Elinor, the older sister in Austen's novel, who believes in putting others first and doing the decent thing. Even though she was two years younger, Sylvia was always trying to set a good example for me. I felt more like Marianne, who made thumping great mistakes for love and fell desperately ill afterwards.

You'd think you wouldn't be able to see any strong likenesses in a newborn baby, but I could. It was astonishing. Like I've said, there was the hair. But the child's long eyes and broad, thick eyebrows were also *exactly* like my sister's. Sylvia's always been proud of her eyebrows. I often caught her stopping to lick a finger and smooth them out in a hallway mirror or pane of glass, or even the reflection in the oven door.

The baby had my sister's mouth, too. That Kewpie-doll bow curled up on each side – you just knew in time those cheeks were going to dent with dimples like Sylvia's. I found this disturbing. Even though I'd been pretty good up till then about not taking any interest in the child.

Knock me out and wake me up when it's over, I told them at the hospital. And when I came round, Sylvia was standing next to the bed with that fat, sleeping little face in her arms.

Without actually saying it, most of us knew by then that Bart and my sister would end up raising the child. At that stage, there wasn't much I could do except give her a name.

Now and then, when they managed to quieten her down, one of them would bring Marianne to me and put her in my arms. But she was restless and heavy, and I grew tired. The more her hair grew and her eyes opened and the dimples began to dent her cheeks, the less I liked seeing her.

We never really had too much to do with each other, my daughter and me. Except in my dreams, where she kept falling overboard into deep lakes and I kept trying to catch her by her long, curly hair.

You know when you put a match to a gas jet? That blue *whumph* as the two elements meet? That's how it feels seeing my sister again. Her voice flares up in me as she strides along the southern end of town, chattering into one of those new portable phones. She's kapping it out so hard she's trotting just short of a run. She's got her hair up in a bun for the heat, and her peasant skirt swirls around her sturdy legs. *Daai meisie*, one of the local farmers said once, *het 'n paar vris bene.*

She stops just outside the wooden gate of the old Papendorf house, where a SOLD sign's been plastered across the crumbling vibracrete. In the muddy driveway, a familiar blue BMW sports car is parked, though the number plate's been changed to SANDILE EC.

Sylvia opens the gate carefully. She does *not* want to be the one who finally breaks it. Not this time. Over the years she's put up with too much teasing about broken wine glasses and shattered dinner plates. Harry's never allowed her to forget the time she snapped the lever of his dental chair clean off.

Up the slasto path, *thump, thump, thump*, Sylvia hurries, her hand already raised to knock. But before she can rap her knuckles against the door, it's wrenched open.

"What do you think?" a man shouts.

Then she's swung up, right off her feet, even though he staggers backwards under the weight.

Last time I saw Sandile Sinto he was sprouting an Afro three times the size of his face. Clearly he's going for more gravitas now. The Afro's been twisted into neat, shoulder-length dreads, and somebody's steady hand has shaved a goatee on his chin. He's ditched the tortoiseshell glasses, too. Instead, almost invisible titanium frames perch on his nose. Until he grins down at Sylvia, and I see that familiar gap-tooth smile, I can hardly believe it's him. But he's as neatly turned out as ever: pressed blue denims and brilliant-white long-sleeved shirt – though there's no tie, and he hasn't fastened the laces of his Reeboks yet.

Sylvia looks around the front hallway and smiles.

In the gloom, Sandile examines her. He takes her hands in his. It's as if he's trying to save her in his memory, just as she is at this moment. Her dimpled smile and chubby legs. Her wild brown hair, already escaping from the bun. For the moment, he doesn't seem too fussed about her old gypsy skirt or the unravelling hem of her blouse.

"I am going to knock this wall out," he swings an arm towards the dark passage behind them, "and open it all up. Then I'm going to have a glass window opening out towards the verandah." He waits for Sylvia to speak.

But Sylvia was always hopeless at homemaking and housekeeping. For a few seconds, she's stumped. "Lots of potential," she says at last, pulling herself together.

Sandile nudges her. "Like you," he grins.

Sylvia gazes towards the kitchen, through the grimy windows to the slab of brittle yellow veld outside. At the bottom of the yard the river muscles past. It glints and reflects on the smoke-stained ceiling of the kitchen. Beyond it, you can see the plot and the yellowwood tree. And beyond that, you can just make out the plumbago growing over the fence, and the back yard of my house.

Sylvia. Still with Sandile Sinto, I see. That always puzzled me. *I* was the one who tumbled into things head over heels. Not you. You were the responsible one. So Harry always said. *Think carefully, Con*, you always told me. *There's always time to think before you speak. Or act.* As if *you* were the older sister, not me.

Ah, but things are still good with you and Sandile, I see. His hand sneaks across your solid waist, turning you towards him to kiss. And you kiss him back, a good long kiss. You unhook the titanium glasses, dangling them in the hands you clasp behind his neck. Sylvia, don't drop them!

Then my sister pulls away. She holds Sandile's face in her hands and pulls his head towards hers, threading her fingers through his dreads.

"Congratulations, Mr Mayor," she smiles.

Long before I got too ill to be interested, it was clear what was happening with Sylvia and Sandile Sinto. We could also all tell the way the wind was blowing for the Scheepersdorp Town Council in the new democratic elections. But I died in 1994, so I had too many other things to think about by then: handing Marianne over to Sylvia and Bart, sorting out my paperwork. Whatever else I may have done wrong, I didn't shirk that.

Of course I left everything to Marianne, under Sylvia and Bart's guardianship. The house had belonged to Sylvia and me since our mother died, and we all decided it would be easiest if Bart stayed there to help Sylvia and Princess with Marianne. Especially since Sylvia was so seldom at home by then.

But the plot behind the house was mine alone. I never completely understood why Ivor's mother Maggie willed that piece of undeveloped land to me, of all people. Maybe she trusted me to do what I thought was right. I certainly tried my best. And I made sure Sylvia understood I was passing that responsibility on to her. I wanted the place to stay as it was. That would take money, of course, but I hoped that, between the two of them, she and Bart might manage not to sell. Naturally, I'd had plenty of offers. Not just because it was a prime piece of land, but also because a lot of people in Scheepersdorp were willing to pay good money to chop down that yellowwood and sort out the bloody parrots once and for all.

At the same time, most people in Scheepersdorp weren't going to give my sister too much grief. Not for a while, in any case. Sylvia had been through a very tough time. And she was only trying to do what her sister had asked her to. People in our town respected that kind of thing.

That, Harry used to say after he'd had a few, was how things worked in Scheepersdorp. People either trusted you or they didn't. If you'd lived there long enough, they helped you even if they didn't trust you. People knew the way of the town.

And if they don't know the way – Harry would raise his fourth highball in a lean, hairy fist – *they'd bladdy well better learn it, hadn't they? Hey? Hey?* And in the bar of the Scheepersdorp Country Club, a circle of pink-flushed faces would nod in agreement, hands holding up an answering circle of glasses. What was good enough for our grandfathers was good enough for us. From the ladies' bar came a set of lipsticked nods.

That was, until Sandile Sinto decided to stand for mayor.

Until Sandile Sinto was *allowed* to stand for mayor.

Here's another surprise: long before he took office, Sandile's photo was up in the Scheepersdorp Country Club. You don't believe me? Take a look. Here, right here: the photographs hanging on the wall of the short passageway leading from the bar to the men's room.

This one of a group of golfers. December 1977. The annual Mayoral Stakes. It was the first year Harry was voted mayor, *and* the day he scored a hole-in-one on the seventh. What a day! Binx Bezuidenhout, the local photographer, was called in. They'd lined up all the golfers in the winning four-ball. Binx was about to take the shot when Harry called the caddies over. What the hell. They'd been good little buggers today. Let them have their picture taken too. *Hau* – Harry turned to his companions and widened his sinewy arms. *Eish*. They could steal the newspaper and show it to their gogos. And the golf team guffawed. One of them slapped Harry on the back.

He was particularly fond of his regular caddy, was Harry. See here? Harry even has a hand on the boy's shoulder. There's evidence, he likes to say – you can see *I* was never a racist.

And this thin boy holding up a five iron from Harry's shiny leather bag. The winning club. Is there something familiar in that tight grin, that shrewd, myopic gaze? Even in third-hand shorts and the faded-to-nothing tee-shirt, it's possible to recognise the gangliness of those limbs, the tight grip of those long, lean fingers.

1977 was a good year for Harry.

1995 clearly isn't.

Chapter 4

ALL ACROSS SCHEEPERSDORP, cast-offs of my life are blossoming. In the post-office queue, a woman has gathered my denim skirt at the waist with a safety pin. Beside her, a child flubbers in my gumboots, three sizes too big. At the taxi rank on Scheepersdorp Square, my straw hat perches on the head of an elderly man as if it's floated down and landed there. There's a circle of dried flowers around the rim. Lavender and pink, and a wire stump where the big silk rose snapped off.

Maybe this will persuade you to protect yourself from the sun, Ivor said, shoving it at me. No wrapping, no birthday card. And who should have known better how I liked flowers in gardens, not on clothes?

Up sails the sun over Scheepersdorp, swallowing shadows as it goes. Rays of light are sliding through the smoke from the mutton braai in the back yard of Sandile Sinto's new house. Music is booming across the valley! It's not even ten a.m., but people are dancing, bottles of Castle held high. Under their bare feet the scorched grass crackles.

What could be more provoking to Harry Healey than this: my sister, the lovely Sylvia, swaying on the back lawn with Sandile

Sinto, mayor elect? One plump arm circled around Sandile's neck, she raises the other to sip from a glass of G and T. Yet still the house over the river and across the plot stays silent.

Alwyn, meanwhile, is burrowing through his mother's linen closet while she's in the kitchen preparing for Marianne. With perfect intuition, his hand locates the whitest, fluffiest bath towel on the shelf. He throws it over his shoulder, avoids the creaking floorboards as he treads carefully down the passage, then lets himself out of the front door and skips down the steps to the gate.

Next door, even though it's not Sunday, Princess has buttoned herself into her red church dress with the white collar. As she bends to strap Marianne into her pram, the starched fabric of the dress crackles. Marianne used to cry when she saw Princess ironing her church dress, but today she just kicks her heels and squeals.

Whenever Princess put that uniform on, she started speaking differently. *I am going now*, she'd say, instead of her usual *Bye, Ma*. And she moved slower too, as if that scrawny frame of hers had suddenly developed height and bulk. Her stockings swished and her court heels clopped as she sailed away from us down the wooden passage.

At the mirror beside the front door, Princess parks the pram to check herself out. She has to stand on tiptoe to get a proper view. Her beret's jammed so tight it squashes her wizened face into an expression that's even more intense. High cheekbones, darting black eyes. Like her hands, they're never still. Watching, planning, dreaming. How often was I forced to listen to those dreams, to what they might mean for me and mine? And just as I was getting into the whole story, or started telling her something *I'd* dreamed, she'd tap an imaginary watch on her knobbly wrist: *I'm sorry Con, I can't stand here with the talking any more. I got too much work.* Now she allows herself a brief, satisfied nod at the trim figure in the mirror and turns to push the pram out of the front door.

There was a time I couldn't have stopped myself from being in there, tangled in the middle of it all. Sandile and Sylvia; Alwyn; Princess; Bart and Marianne. If I were still alive, I'd be dancing beside Sylvia on Sandile's arid lawn by now. Or pushing open the wire gate of Harry's back yard to jog up the dirt path and find out for myself what was going on in there. Into the lion's den. Maybe I'd take one of the other paths across the plot. This one, for instance. I used to fly along it three or four times a day. I knew every inch of soil, every plant and stone and bulb from our back gate to the back gate of number fourteen Bloubessie Way. Ivor's house.

Ivor and Janice's house now.

Only three people alive who'll remember the other path worn from Ivor's back gate. The one leading down to the yellowwood tree. I'm pretty sure nobody would've walked it in the last year. Why would they want to? But I know where its scar still lies. Blurred by verbena and blackjacks and buffalo grass. Disguised, but still stored in the soil's memory. Like a word written over and over and underlined on a piece of cheap blue notepaper. *Sorry. Sorry sorry <u>sorry</u>.*

"Hullo?" Sylvia says. God knows how she managed to hear her portable phone over the boom box on Sandile's back stoep, but she stops dancing and sticks a finger in one ear, receiver to the other. Then she glances across at Sandile, about to pull the cap off another Castle. Her broad shoulders slump.

"I'll come with you," Sandile says.

Is that a good idea? Never mind. Too late. A minute later, the two of them are running down the banked lawn towards the barbed-wire fence and the river at the bottom. Sandile stoops to stretch the fence wide for Sylvia to climb through, then follows.

Sylvia's one of only a handful of people confident enough to take this shortcut across the plot. She wouldn't dream of suggesting she and Sandile approach Harry's house from the front gate off Plumbago Way. After all, Sandile himself is not quite used to being ushered through the front doors of Scheepersdorp homes. Not yet.

It wasn't that long ago, for instance, that Alwyn's mother, Esmé van der Walt, only served Sandile tea from a special mug. The same one she keeps for her sixty-year-old "garden boy". Even now, on the rare occasions Sandile visits Alwyn, Esmé spends a good ten minutes disinfecting the cup once the front door has closed behind their visitor.

Watch them go! Across the river Sylvia and Sandile swing on the rope hanging from the fig tree. They may be nearing thirty, but they've been doing this since they were five. Harry tied the thick hessian ropes there for us – one from the wild peach tree on the plot side of the river, the other from the fig tree on the bank at Papendorf's. He spent a whole day showing Alwyn and Sylvia and me how to take a running start from the river bank, grab the rope between our hands and feet and sail over. Of course, old Papendorf tried protesting – especially when Harry let Sandile join the fun – but he never stood a chance against Harry.

Sylvia couldn't care less about her skirt riding up over her thighs, or the strained bow of the massive branch. But Sandile has misgivings. Particularly when the old tree is heard to groan under Sylvia's weight. One of his first tasks as mayor will be to build a pedestrian bridge across the river bordering his property. He lands lightly on the opposite bank, on the path leading through the plot – although that, too, is slowly being erased by lantana and buffalo grass.

Sandile and Sylvia know the way through it well enough. Sylvia in the lead, they stride towards the yellowwood tree, then veer right, around the patch of khaki bush, towards where the Port Jacksons have seeded near Harry's back gate, rusted shut. Sandile tries shifting it, but in the end it takes a vigorous klap from Sylvia's broad hand to make it budge.

Through Harry's orchard the two of them trot, Sylvia still well ahead. Past the plum and apricot trees, the pecan-nut trees (shabbier than when I saw them last) and the small mound beneath them with a carved wooden sign: *Soapy 1980–1993*. As they reach the back steps of the stoep, the dogs inside the house start to tjank. But a bellow from the lounge silences them.

Chapter 5

"WATCH HERE, CONNIE WEST!" he roared, and at the sound of his voice the parrots ripped up from the yellowwood tree. "I am the mayor of Scheepersdorp!"

It was one of Harry's good days. He'd just been voted mayor for the third time running, and won the Scheepersdorp and District Golf Championships. With one hand he vaulted over his back gate onto the plot, Soapy sailing beside him. She may not have had flocks of sheep to herd, but keeping up with Harry was a perfect substitute. When they landed on the path, clouds of dust powdered up under Soapy's paws and Harry's slim feet. He grinned as I applauded from our stoep across the way.

It was different on the bad days. When the parrots stripped his pecan trees clean; when the council vetoed his decision to use the school playground as a helicopter landing strip for his business trips. Or simply when the murky mood settled on him. It was like charcoal clouds from a pile of burning rubber that had been set alight by someone far away. Someone who knew something about him the rest of us couldn't possibly understand.

You could never tell who the blame would finally settle on.

Whoever it was, it was no use hiding. Sooner or later the call would go out and you'd be found. It was almost a relief when you were.

Sometimes the message would be delivered by phone, or Princess or Phineas the gardener would come to ferret you out: *The mayor he say he want to see you now. He's waiting there by his house.*

Once Harry had you standing in front of him, shifting from leg to leg, he'd start. Everything was awful and terrible and beyond repair. And it had all been started by you. Yes, you! Some small thing you hadn't been aware of. How could you be so stupid? Didn't you know you were killing him? You were killing all of them! Or simply this: did you know you were a complete disappointment from the moment you stole your first breath?

I just wanted to tell you that you are:

A failure.

An embarrassment.

An utter disgrace to the whole of Scheepersdorp.

When he said it he sounded sad. Usually he had his head in his hands. But somehow he always made sure his diction was perfectly clear. He wouldn't want you misunderstanding anything. At the same time, he seemed so genuinely wretched you almost wanted to pat him on the back.

Sylvia and I had heard it all over the years. What could we do? You didn't become tougher the more those things got said. Repeat something often enough and people *will* start to believe.

At the same time, Sylvia was always a bit cleverer than I was. It never took long for me to react. I'd flame back, give Harry as good as I got. Maybe because she was younger, Sylvia got to watch and figure out for herself what wouldn't work with him. Her strategy was just to listen. Sometimes her head would droop, like a pack horse being loaded.

And another thing, Sylvia West. He'd dig more and more

34

frantically for stuff to pile on, desperate to tip the balance till she'd finally explode and take him on. Loitering protectively outside the lounge door in Harry's passage, I'd hear my sister slap him into place with one short, sharp sentence: *Will you stop it, Uncle Harry, now!* And then: *It's like there's a poison in you that's got to come out!*

You could see he felt better after that. Things would improve rapidly once Sylvia lost her patience with him. Especially if he got her to cry. *Then* he was sorry, Sylvia, so very, very sorry. He hadn't meant it. He was only joking! *Can't you take a joke? How about we all go down to Royal Hotel for a milkshake later?* Raising his voice loud enough for me to hear in the passageway, *Go tell that sister of yours to scrub herself up. Tell her to wash her face, man. We'll put her on the back of the bakkie and she can come too.*

Within minutes, Harry would be out in his orchard again, whistling away while he waited for us to get ready. And Sylvia and I would be walking slowly home across the plot.

I never stood for it. *I* never took it all on or gave in so easily. Not on the surface anyway. But just because I wasn't afraid to shout back doesn't mean Harry never hit the mark. He was a genius at that.

Sylvia raps her knuckles loudly against Harry's kitchen door. A futile exercise, as the yapping from inside alerted everyone long ago. Almost immediately, the door swings open on Harry's wife Letty. Poor Letty. Here she is, nearing sixty, looking the same as she's always done. Still in the same old flowered house apron, grey hair pulled back in a thick bun. Still pretending she can control the two Maltese poodles snapping at Sandile's heels.

"Come in," a voice moans from the far end of the house.

No need for Sylvia to ask where Harry is. Even if she didn't already know, you could scoop up bucketfuls of the outrage pulsing

35

down the passageway from the lounge. Along the wooden passage she stomps with bare, dirty feet. Past the gallery of Harry's mayoral pictures and the wallpaper curling from decades of heat. *Tinkle tinkle*, tremble the sherry glasses in the drinks cabinet in the lounge, set off by Sylvia's sturdy footsteps.

She's managed to persuade Sandile to wait in the kitchen with Letty for the moment. Sandile, who is no stranger to this house. Over the years he has painted every wall and sanded every window frame. Even now, as Sylvia marches up the passage on her own, Sandile is ambling over to Letty's kitchen window to check the putty on the panes he helped install twelve years ago. With Harry, you get nothing for free.

In the doorway of the lounge, Sylvia waits for Harry to notice her.

He's crouched, as usual, in the La-Z-Boy opposite the TV, head in hands. As if he hadn't heard her coming long ago. The lounge curtains have finally been pulled open and bars of spanspek-yellow sun are raking across the carpet towards Harry's veldskoens. Beside them, a Checkers bag spills pecan nuts. You can see it's been flung down as Harry dropped into the chair. Even though she's been dead for almost two years now, Soapy's dog basket is still lying in the corner beside the bookcase.

Tap, *tap*, *tap* rustles the pecan-nut tree at the window. Everyone wants Harry's gaze to shine on them. If only for a moment.

We used to believe Harry was the strongest man in the world, a cross between Captain Haddock and Desperate Dan. To a child, his gigantic head seemed five times bigger than his tense, lithe body. In reality, when Sylvia and I had grown to our full heights of five foot five and six, we were only slightly shorter than him. But Harry was masterful at making things appear bigger than they were. Especially when those piercing blue eyes glared down at you as he drilled, or fastened braces so tight that nobody except him would ever get them off again.

Kyk daai tande, he'd boom at visitors, shoving Sylvia and me forward and ordering us to grin. *Those perfect teeth didn't happen by accident, you know!* For a long time, he was dead set on sorting Sandile out, too: that gap between his front teeth was a personal affront. *It's for your own good, man!* Harry would yell. But – not for the first time – Sandile refused to be bullied. He'd heard what happened in Harry's surgery.

"Everyone," – Harry finally clears his throat – "is talking about you, Sylvia. I am deeply disappointed in you." His pronunciation, as usual, is perfect. "What would your mother say?"

"About what?" Sylvia asks.

"You, and this—" Harry shifts his hands, as if the weight of his head is too great to bear. "This. Those. People over there." Finally he lifts his head. "What kind of a bladdy racket is that?"

Only a year since I saw him last, the strong outlines of his face have frayed, skin yellowing like old newspaper. It's as if somebody's rubbed at a graphite drawing, blurring the lines. His curly dark hair has receded even further, and more brushes of grey have appeared at the temples. The pouches under his eyes have sagged deeper, too. You'd think that might make him look softer, but it only makes you notice more the laser glare of his eyes and the sharpness of his craggy nose. "If we ever had a parrot braai," Alwyn said once, pissed, "we could hook Harry onto the spit with his nose."

"Uncle Harry," Sylvia says, "you and Auntie Letty have golf parties that go on till two in the morning here. Nobody says anything about *that*."

"Sylvia, Sylvia." Harry shakes his head. "Those people are breaking every rule in the book. Noise. Pollution." He ticks them off on sturdy fingers. "Sacrificing sheep in the back yard."

"What sheep? Nobody's sacrificing a sheep!"

37

"Not yet," Harry yells, "but don't tell me they're not planning to. If I were still mayor I'd get the health inspectors out!"

Sylvia sighs. "Is *that* what you wanted to see me about?"

"Shit," Harry groans like he's been kneed. "Do you have any idea what you're doing to me, Sylvia? Do you *know* what people are saying about you?"

Harry used to tell us he had sleepless nights about Sylvia and me. From the day our mother died and he was made guardian, the two of us got reports on how Harry had slept the night before (not a wink), how his back was feeling (broken) and his general health (ropey). All of it due to us.

So what's the alternative? I'd snapped back one day. By then even *he* didn't have the nerve to argue with me.

Despite all those sleepless nights, Harry never seemed to age. Maybe hammering and sawing and swearing and bullying were the secrets of eternal youth. Except, over the past few years, we'd noticed a change. That beer boep he couldn't quite master had started to unbalance his normally lean, coordinated body. What once had been a sprint became a trot. Glasses seemed incongruous perched on that Roman nose. And of course there was the avalanche of pills next to his bed. Myprodol, Duphalac, Valium.

He's thinner now, too. Except for the pot belly getting in the way when he shifts to the edge of the La-Z-Boy, stabbing his finger at my sister to make his point.

Listen to me now, Connie West. I know you're not going to listen, but LISTEN.

"Christ, Sylvia!" Harry hisses. "It's time you *did* something with your life, man! Twenty-eight years old and you're still filing maintenance contracts for Toppie de Bruyn. Is *that* what you want to do with the rest of your life?

"And what happened to going to secretarial college in PE?" he blasts on. "Hey? Two years ago you promised you'd go. I *told* you I'd pay for it. Man, I even got Toppie to chip in. That poor, desperate bastard. And what happens? Nothing. *Nothing.*"

It was Harry who'd found Sylvia the job at Toppie de Bruyn's. He'd just about *ordered* Toppie to take Sylvia on. Once she'd started there, Harry loved stopping by our house after golf on Saturdays to tell Sylvia and me how Toppie had been complaining again. Sylvia filed things in all the wrong places. She wore laddered stockings to work and ate tuna sandwiches when clients were in the waiting room.

"I've told you," Sylvia says, "I never wanted to be a secretary."

"What are you gonna do then, hey? Hey? You can't just live off other people for the rest of your life, you know. You're going to need a practical qualification."

Sylvia considers. "How about plumbing?" she asks eventually.

"Jesus Christ, Sylvia."

"Pinky Botha needs someone. He told me last week."

"Don't be funny with me now."

"I'm *not* being funny. I mean. What's wrong with being Pinky's apprentice? Pinky wouldn't mind. I'm strong enough. And it's got to be better than working for Toppie de Bruyn."

"And another thing," – Harry was never stumped for long – "when are you going to do something about that piece of land, young lady?"

"Oh." Sylvia's sleepy brown eyes widen. She folds her arms behind her back. "Are we talking about the plot now? What's bothering you, Uncle Harry?"

"What's *bothering* me?" Harry slams his palms down onto the leather arms of the La-Z-Boy. "*I'll* tell you what's effing bothering me! Bloody weeds and duwweltjies seeding themselves all over my garden. Rats and moles and God knows what else burrowing through my rubbish bins. Those bladdy birds are eating all my pecan nuts. *Look* at that!" Harry stabs a trembling finger at the packet on the floor. "*That* is all I've managed to salvage since yesterday! I have grown those pecans for five years and those birds come down and flatten it in two hours. And the noise! Jesus Christ! Let me tell you," – the vein on Harry's forehead looks ready to burst – "let me tell *you*, my girl! I could have the bloody *council* on you!" And when Sylvia still doesn't respond: "People are going to get *tick-bite fever* walking through that place! Those rats are carrying *bubonic plague* around this town! You have let me down, Sylvia," he groans. "I am bitterly disappointed in you."

"Doc Healey."

Neither of them noticed Sandile ambling up the passage, but now he's standing in the doorway behind Sylvia, a good head taller than she is, hands clasped behind his back. A ray of sun glances off his glasses, making it impossible to see his eyes.

My little shadow, Harry used to call him all those years ago. Back in the days when Sandile dogged Harry's every step. *Hand me the hammer. Go fetch the ragged-tooth saw. Not that one, the one in the workshop, man. Go fetch the pellet gun. The sandpaper. The driving wedge. Go fetch the bullets and the .22. Move it.*

"What do you want?" Harry glares at him.

"Connie loved that place, Uncle Harry," Sylvia says.

Ah. Connie.

For a few seconds all three allow themselves to be caught up in their own thoughts. Sandile gazes out of the window at the pecan-nut trees. Sylvia looks at Harry.

Harry is staring at the carpet.

I have slaved my guts out for you and that sister of yours, Connie West. And what do I get for it? Nothing. NOTHING.

Not nothing, Uncle Harry. You get to watch us cock things up so you can fix them again.

Jesus. Where did you learn to talk like that?

"Uncle Harry," says Sylvia eventually, "you know how Connie loved the plants there. And the … wildlife."

Even though she's careful not to say "parrots", it's as if one's just swooped into the room. Sylvia hurries on: "She wanted me to take care of the plot, and I promised her I'd try. The thing is, that piece of land's just sitting there now. And like you say, it's getting out of hand. I can't afford to have it cleaned up every month. Honestly, it's just becoming a big las for me. At least if I built a house I could rent it out."

Hard to tell if Harry's listening, still staring at the carpet like that. Sylvia puffs out her cheeks, waiting. Sandile hooks off his glasses and starts polishing the thick lenses on the corner of his white tee-shirt. "Or," Sylvia tries again, "I could just put it up for sale. As a last resort."

Still Harry doesn't respond. The beat from across the river ripples into the room, setting the glasses in the drinks cabinet trembling again. When Harry looks up, Sandile is smiling at him. The gap in his teeth flashes triumphantly.

"Go on," says Harry at last. "Bugger off. Both of you." He bats a limp hand at his visitors. "I was mayor of this town for twenty years," he mutters as they trail down the passage to the kitchen, through the back door and into the heat again. "You can't tell me I don't know what's going on here."

It's an unsatisfactory ending. Harry back with his head in his hands, waiting for Letty to come and notice him. Sylvia and Sandile making their way down the path towards Harry's back gate. No slamming doors. No tears. No threats never to see each other again. Never to talk. No *That's it. It's over. I'm leaving my money to the Scheepersdorp Golf Academy.*

Good.

And don't come crying to me when you need help.

41

I won't.

Fine.

Fine.

FINE.

That was always more my way than Sylvia's.

Back in the kitchen, Letty pushes her palm on the kitchen table to stand. In some ways, not having children saved her a lot of stress. Harry wouldn't have taken easily to competition. Down the passage to the lounge she trots.

She's not the only one feeling sorry for Harry now. Perhaps he'd feel better if he could hear Sylvia. Lifting the wire latch on Harry's back gate, she turns to Sandile: "Maybe he's got a point. Maybe it *is* time I did something about the plot."

Chapter 6

"WHAT IS THE POINT," demanded Harry, "of giving an eighteen-year-old girl an undeveloped plot of land?"

Why did Maggie do it? Harry was genuinely baffled. Hurt, even. *He* could have told her what to do. He could have helped her. Hell, he would've done it *for* her, she knew that. As mayor, Harry had a duty to all his neighbours. As Scheepersdorp's only dentist, he knew the full extent of their root-canal work and receding gums. Once he had you tipped back in that chair of his, he could bombard you with advice and ideas until you left numbed in jaw and mind. Maggie Shepherd had been no different. So we all thought. I was often around when Harry brought plums and apricots from his orchard over to Maggie and dished out advice about bringing up Ivor. What a boy needs. Was I the only one who noticed how politely Maggie listened? How she never laughed at Harry's jokes like the rest of us?

Still, even I couldn't have predicted Maggie's will. I wasn't even suspicious when Toppie de Bruyn called all four of us down to his offices two days after Maggie's funeral. We all thought, what with Ivor being under age, Harry would be made guardian. Or trustee. Even though Maggie never seemed to care whether he visited her or not, he was the only person in Scheepersdorp who ever did. As for Sylvia and me, Harry said Maggie owned a couple of fine pieces of jewellery, and she'd always enjoyed the company of her son's friends.

You could have fooled me.

After all, Harry expanded, steering the red bakkie down Main Road – *after all, Maggie was very fond of you. You know that, don't you?* Sylvia and I were squashed beside him in the cab, and Ivor was standing on the back of the truck. As usual it was Sylvia who smiled and nodded yes. I was too busy watching Harry from the corner of my eye. His right elbow was crooked out the window but his eyes were churning with ideas: the house, the plot, the children; education and development. A practice for Ivor once he'd qualified. And not forgetting a new car for himself, Harry. Also, that twelve-bore rifle he'd always wanted. And an Aberdeen bull. He could keep it on the plot. Clear out all the other crap and plant lucerne there. Cut down the yellowwood so the parrots would finally go somewhere else to feed. Make a fine table from the timber, too. Of course it would take a couple of weeks to get it all done. Less if he hired a prison gang.

Ivor stood on the back of the bakkie, facing the traffic with Soapy in his arms. She must have been only about six weeks old then. Ivor's sandy hair streamed back in the wind, laying his face bare. He wasn't frowning or smiling, and his eyes gave nothing away. I wished I could tell what he was thinking.

Even when Toppie finally started reading the will, Ivor's face showed nothing. I mean, she'd been his mother, after all. He sat with Soapy on his lap, stroking the white diamond on her forehead.

I'd had no idea what to expect. Turns out, none of us did. At first, it seemed Harry was right. Maggie's house and the bulk of her estate went into a trust fund for Ivor, to be administered by

Toppie and Harry. Then, as predicted, there was a bit of jewellery for Sylvia and me.

The first surprise came when Toppie read out that Maggie Shepherd had willed her entire library to me. Harry nodded approvingly. This was no small gift. Maggie's lounge and dining room (and, as I was to discover later, bedroom) were crammed floor to ceiling with books she'd either inherited or bought. Fiction, non-fiction, art and poetry: there were books on every topic you could imagine. Sometimes, while I was waiting for Ivor to pull on his veldskoens or make himself a sandwich, I'd choose a book from one of the shelves and sit cross-legged on the lounge floor. Until Maggie's will got read out, I never realised she'd even noticed me.

I was still getting over that one when Toppie moved on to the plot.

"To be administered in trust by the aforementioned Harold Healey until she turns twenty-one," – you could tell Toppie was nervous by the way he tried making his voice as dry and professional as possible – "I bequeath my property in Scheepersdorp, erf 6453, to Constance Ivy West."

"Good God." Harry reddened. He glared at Toppie. "That's going to make life difficult."

Toppie was struggling to keep up. It was difficult to shift out of the role of Harry's drinking buddy at the Scheepersdorp Country Club.

"Jesus," Harry sighed. His gaze settled on me.

I opened my mouth. Sylvia kicked me under the table and I shut it again.

On the way home none of us spoke. Instead of standing face-on to the traffic, Ivor sat with his back to the cab, hands dangling between his knees and Soapy curled beside him. I wondered what he'd made of it all, though I knew better than to ask.

I kept thinking about Maggie. I hadn't spent more than five minutes at a time with her. She'd grown up in Scheepersdorp herself, and come back here after she divorced Ivor's dad. As far as I could tell, she looked after Ivor, made sure he had food and clothes and stuff. I don't know what they talked about when they were alone together. When I was around, she didn't seem to care what Ivor and I did, so long as we did it outside. Most days she kept indoors, smoking and reading and knitting until evening came. She must have seen us roaming around the Kanonkop and the river and the plot that bordered all our gardens. Come to think of it, I do remember glimpsing her at the kitchen window every now and then. Just her long, silvery-dark hair and the smoke wreathing up the windows.

There was a good wide view down to the river from her kitchen window, and she would have seen us swinging across and catching spiders and lizards in the branches of the trees. Sometimes I wondered if she wouldn't mind escaping and joining us there.

Chapter 7

Ten-thirty. The sun is ratcheting up its heat. A giant shadow whips across the outside wall of the kitchen. As if a blade's ripped open a sack of flour, they finally pour out of the sky. *Oppas, hier kom hulle!*

How is it possible to make such a racket with just a tongue and a leathery beak? It's like a hundred galvanised buckets are being rattled with wooden sticks. It even drowns out the party music from Sandile's house.

From the roots up, the yellowwood starts to shudder. Speeding lozenges of viridian and alizarin are barrelling into the mass of needled leaves.

There used to be hundreds of them, once, nesting in the yellowwood forest on the other side of the Kop. On a still day, we'd hear them screeching in the distance. But when the local farmers started chopping down the trees, the parrots came searching further afield. They'd swoop down from the Kop so the sky darkened over Scheepersdorp, and in seconds they'd be all over the yellowwood in the plot and Harry's pecan-nut trees. Harry's pot-shots hardly made a dent in them, then. Still, over the years, their numbers grew smaller and smaller. For a start, there weren't enough yellowwood fruits and pecan nuts for all of them, let alone Harry. And then pecans weren't their natural food. Alwyn told me the parrots had developed a disease from all that unhealthy eating. He'd rescued one or two from Harry's orchard and taken them down to the SPCA.

Now it looks like there can't be more than eighty left. They still make a decent racket, though. And they still manage to get right into the heart of the trembling tree. When they screw their heads 360 degrees to get at the fruit, it's like a spanner tightening a bolt.

From the back lawn of Alwyn's house, his mother Esmé stops to glare at the yellowwood, hands on tightly corseted hips. Oh, the stiff perm of that blue-rinsed crown! The relentless pink check of the housecoat! Esmé screws up her sagging face – first at the tree, then at Marianne, babbling happily where she's been placed on a blanket on the grass. Although Marianne seems perfectly content, Esmé lumbers towards her, soothing and muttering, flourishing a freshly baked rusk. But Marianne is on her feet and toddling away, towards the back fence to get a better look at the birds.

Across the plot at number fourteen, Janice Shepherd reaches for her earplugs and pulls the kitchen curtains shut.

The first time Janice heard the parrots, she called the police. That's how the rest of us knew she'd slept over at Ivor's house after the dance at the Scheepersdorp Museum. Ivor had been called out early for an emergency caesar, and Janice woke up alone at his house to the caterwauling from what she thought was Ivor's back yard. She told us afterwards she thought some-one was being murdered.

I was awake early – in fact, I'd been up most of the night –

and I looked out of my kitchen window that morning to see a pot-bellied constable sweating across the plot towards the yellowwood. He was banging on a dustbin lid to try to move them on. Fat chance.

The scene struck me as a fitting metaphor for the situation between Ivor and Janice and me. The one I'd been raking over all night. Someone chasing parrots out of my yellowwood tree.

Today, in the workshop at the back of his house, Harry doesn't even look up as the birds sweep in. Even with the scream of the lathe, it's not like he'd miss the familiar screeching three hundred metres away. It's only a matter of time before they head his way.

Sprinting the last short stretch down to the river, Sylvia and Sandile glance back. One at a time, they grab the rope and swing over to the other side, away from the ear-splitting shrieks.

In and out of Harry's lathe the plank glides. The pellet gun and the .22 rifle are nowhere in sight. They stay where they are, locked away in the safe under his bed. And the key for the safe, as everyone in Scheepersdorp knows, is in the third drawer of the dresser below the TV in the lounge.

Like someone drugged, Harry pushes the plank in, catches it on the other side. Then he feeds it in again. He looks like he could carry on doing that till the plank's skimmed right down to paper.

It's confusing, is what it is.

I could have been so many things. I could have gone to Rhodes University and studied English. I probably should have. It would have been a big fight to get Harry to hand over my inheritance money for a BA, but both of us would have gone into the ring wanting me to win.

I could have been a teacher. Or a lawyer. According to Harry, I might have made a decent farmer's wife. I had a way with plants, he admitted grudgingly.

Man. You've got green fingers, no question. But Jeez, Constance. It's not very attractive the way you mess around in those old gardening pants. Put on a nice dress, man. Comb your hair. No man is going to marry a woman who doesn't make an effort with herself. You look like someone's put rotting fish under your nose. Smile. Why can't you just smile?

After matric, I got a job at Bakkies Coetzee's nursery behind the garage on Main Road. To make a bit extra I took cuttings and raised saplings I sold to Bakkies and the local farmers, along with bulbs and some vegetables I grew at home.

Not smiling and wearing old gardening pants came in useful when dealing with the farmers around Scheepersdorp. In the end they forgot who I was and started treating me like one of them. When I started cultivating citrus trees and ran out of space, Bakkies eventually sold the nursery to me. I wasn't too unhappy with how things happened. I was making a fair living, and I didn't feel ready to leave Scheepersdorp. A lot of that – well, I was hanging around because of Ivor. Waiting for him to qualify and come home, I suppose.

Whatever free time I had I spent either reading or down at the plot. Maybe that's when Maggie Shepherd saw me, looking out of her back window while she waited for the kettle to boil. I was always taking slips or separating bulbs, or planting new ones I'd picked up on my trips to the Kop. Maybe Maggie even watched me watering the knee-high sapling I discovered in the long grass one day. I knew one of the parrots must have seeded it there.

Harry was almost as excited as I was when I was stupid enough to show him six months later. By then the tree was already over a metre tall. He gazed down at it, hands on hips.

Makes beautiful wood, he said. *When it gets big enough we could make a dining-room suite.*

After a couple of years, fruit began to appear. The parrots weren't far behind. And it didn't take them long to discover that the pecans in Harry's orchard were a short flight away.

It got so bad that when Harry heard the birds coming he'd run to the bedroom to get the .22. He tried teaching Alwyn to use it, but Alwyn's aim was always wide, though I'm pretty sure he faked it. None of us could make Alwyn do something he didn't want to, but he never enjoyed standing up to anyone, let alone Harry. In any case, nothing put those parrots off. Letty never did get to make the pecan pie Harry hankered after.

I was in senior school at the time. Every day when I got home from class I'd run down the long passage to the kitchen window to check if the yellowwood was still there. Harry could so easily have hacked it out when I was away, but he never did.

He tried everything else, though. *Listen to me, young lady. Man, this tree is going to grow so big you'll never get it out of here. This is a town, for Chrissake.* He threatened to make Sylvia and me move in with him and Letty if I didn't cut the tree down. He threatened to cut my allowance off. Not to pay my school fees. When the plot became mine, he even tried buying the tree from me. He started the bidding at R100, to be paid off in annual instalments, and woke Toppie from his Sunday-afternoon nap to come draw the contract up. As usual, Toppie took it all way too seriously.

Harry could talk till he was blue in the face, and he usually did. It wasn't pleasant to cope with that barrage of abuse, but I had watched that tree grow, and I wasn't going to let Harry take it away from me.

Almost as if it was showing its gratitude, the tree grew furry and fat over time. So portly you could hide yourself in the middle, deep enough for Harry not to find you there. You could hide letters and packets of stolen cigarettes and condoms and bottles of homemade pineapple beer.

And I still enjoyed it when the parrots swept in. Yes, the noise was deafening. But it never lasted that long, and it seemed to me things were working out the way they ought to. Parrots and yellowwood trees belonged together. And I'd made it possible. The parrots had put the tree there and I'd kept it for them.

So what if Esmé van der Walt complained she couldn't sleep? The parrots had become the sound of Scheepersdorp. Their chattering and screeching reminded me of Esmé's coffee mornings. Or Princess shouting across the road to her friends in Xhosa, saying things I itched to understand. What was she saying about me? About Marianne and Bart? Why did she have to shout so loudly? Princess told me once it was so everybody could hear what she was saying. So they would know she wasn't skindering about them.

Chapter 8

"ALL I CAN TELL YOU," the Boatman says, "is you will know this thing when you see it. And you must be finished by half past six."

We're standing on my front stoep, and his eyes keep flicking past me towards Ivor's house or Alwyn's place, or the centre of town where the Saturday-morning crowds are starting to pour out of taxis into Scheepersdorp Square. He shoots out a wrist to show me his watch: ten minutes past eleven.

The sun bakes down on Alwyn, now striding towards the town square in his blue denims and white tee, towel around his neck. Light sparkles on Princess's red umbrella, bobbing through the crowd two blocks behind him.

The Boatman's so tall he looms over me, but it doesn't feel threatening. Perhaps because he seems more irritable than angry. He's ditched the Carducci suit for an open-neck golf shirt and casual slacks, and loafers that look pretty high class. His hair's trimmed close to his scalp now, a neat, greying scrub. And he's pushed his sunglasses up over his head so I can see his almond-shaped eyes. They remind me of the Byzantine portraits in one of the art books Maggie left me.

"I must take you back half past six," the Boatman says again.

He sticks his jaw out like he's expecting me to argue. He doesn't seem to notice the red-black stain seeping through the blue fabric on the left of his chest. Finally he says: "Don't look in the obvious places."

"What?" I'm still staring at the sticky mess on his chest.

"I said: don't look in the obvious places, Ms West. That is why you are here. It is all I can tell you. You must look at *all* these things."

Then he's down among the crowd on the town square, weaving his way towards where Princess has almost caught up with Alwyn.

Soon they're side by side: the tall, gangly young man and the petite, neatly dressed woman. They're headed for the road leading towards the bridge over the river and the N1.

Don't look in the obvious places. I hug my knees and sit tight, safe on my front stoep. Sunlight sifts through the leaves of the dipladenia I planted under a trellis shortly before I took to my bed for the last time. I lean back on the cast-iron chair with the wobbly leg I'd always meant to get repaired.

On a day like today I came out to sit in the sun, in pyjamas and dressing gown and the sheepskin slippers Bart bought in East London for me. Someone came and put the baby in my arms. She was heavy, and her hair brushed against my cheeks. She kicked against me so powerfully I almost fell back. I was pretty weak by then. When she took my knuckle to her mouth it felt slimy and hot. She was too restless and they had to take her away from me again. They were only trying to be nice.

They did their best, Sylvia and Bart. The child cried night and day, so they kept her from me. Most days, Princess would take her down to the plot, far enough away from my bedroom for her screaming to reach me as just a thin mosquito-like whine.

I get up and walk towards the far corner of the stoep. I'm in my old gardening shorts and takkies now, and my tee-shirt from Harry that says *Scheepersdorp Golf Academy*. I've got my hair scraped back in a bun, and scratches across my face and hands from cutting back the bougainvillea over the kitchen pergola. At the top of the steps I lean out and listen to the front door of number fourteen Bloubessie Way slamming shut. I can just make out Ivor's head and shoulders as he skips down the polished green steps, black holdall in hand.

I won't go nearer. I don't *have* to go nearer, or even look, to know the route he'll take to the surgery on Main Road. I know the crackle his crisp white coat – so beautifully starched and ironed – will make as he walks. And I know who's cleaning up the house behind him. I can see the blur of her head across the windows as she trots in and out from kitchen to dining room.

The first thing I ever said to Ivor was: *Hey. Pick that up. This is not a rubbish dump.*

I was standing on the top step of my back stoep in slippers and jeans. He'd just dropped a stompie on our lawn and was busy grinding it out with his heel. He was already turned to go home, but when I called out he jumped and turned around. It was about two a.m. and all the house lights were off, so even though the moon was full it took him a few seconds to make out where I was. Maybe he thought it was a cheek. At school they'd told us to make him feel at home, him being new in town and all that. His parents were divorced, they said, in the same tone they spoke about cancer or nervous breakdowns. Well, Sylvia and I knew all about that kind of stuff. We'd never known our father, and since our mother had died the year before, we'd been on our own. With a lot of help from Harry Healey, of course.

Sylvia would never have said anything about the stompie.

She'd have come back later and picked it up herself before Harry or Princess found out one of us was smoking. But Sylvia had already gone to bed. Before I came outside, I stuck my head in the door of her room and saw her asleep, her dance dress dumped on the floor with her silver heels and handbag thrown aside like there'd been an explosion.

I don't know why she asked Ivor to go to the standard-eight dance with her. Maybe she felt sorry for him. Sylvia always noticed if people were left out or lame.

I thought he'd left already. I'd been hanging around inside, reading, while I waited for him to leave, kiss my sister goodnight or whatever else it was he wanted to do with her, so I could finally lock up. Sylvia and I were trying hard to show Harry we could live on our own so we wouldn't have to move in with him and Letty.

When he finally made out where I was, Ivor picked up the stompie without saying a word and shoved it in the pocket of the tux he'd borrowed from Alwyn van der Walt. The hems of the trousers had been rolled up about three times and tacked into place, whether by Ivor or his mother Maggie I can't say.

The *doef-doef* of the disco from the school hall had stopped long ago. Once or twice a jackal howled from beyond the Kop and a sheep bleated from one of the smallholdings.

What did a town boy make of all this?

I was curious, I suppose. That's why I dared him.

I said, "It's much quicker for you to get home that way," and nodded at the gate from our back yard leading onto the plot. "I can show you if you want."

The piece of land belonged to his mother, after all. We all assumed one day it would be his. Before Ivor could change his mind, I ran inside to pull on my sheepskin jacket and gumboots. Then I headed down the lawn to the back gate, frost crunching under my feet. At the gate I unlatched the clasp and held it back for him to follow me.

He was only slightly taller than me, trim enough to have to use the first notch on Alwyn's belt. He had a strange build. Sometimes I thought it looked like the wrong limbs had been sewn onto his body. His chest and belly were so long and sinewy, they just didn't seem to fit with his stocky arms and legs. And yet, when you got to his round, solemn face, it all made perfect sense. His hair was a mousy blond and his eyes were no particular shade of blue, but somehow when you put it all together, there was something magnetic about him. Maybe because he took himself so seriously, everyone else did too.

"So?" he asked when I stopped halfway down the path, twenty metres short of the yellowwood tree. "Do I turn off here?"

"Yes," I said. My breath billowed into the cold air. In the moonlight, Ivor eyed me calmly. I pointed towards his house, the brickwork silhouetted in the silvery light eighty metres to our right. A yellow glow from Maggie's bedroom window flickered through the branches of the acacias on the plot.

"We're halfway to the river now," I said. "You want to carry on?"

I could see he wanted to say no, but he didn't know how. In any case, I didn't give him a chance. Before he could say a word I ducked under a euphorbia and headed for the river bank. At that stage, there was no path cleared from Ivor's back gate to the yellowwood tree. Not that you could have made out a path clearly, even with a full moon. But I could find my way across that piece of land blindfolded.

I tried not to disturb the spiderwebs looped across the khaki bush and rhus running along the old path. I'd always felt the place belonged to them more than it belonged to us. I kept holding back branches for Ivor and telling him where to step

57

next. The only time he hesitated was when I stopped next to the river at the wild peach tree.

"This is where the night adders nest," I said. He must have sensed I wasn't joking. "They won't bother you if you don't bother them." I'd already climbed into the low V of the tree to grab hold of the rope.

The river was flowing fast from the Kop. Normally it was no wider than three metres, but the winter snows had fattened it. In daylight it was the colour of malt beer, but at night it was silver-backed, streaked with moonlight. Close by, the rushing noise shut out almost everything else.

When I swung across, I liked closing my eyes. That was my best moment: hanging there in the darkness, the water whooshing beneath me. It was like I'd been scooped up and taken out of life for a bit. Till I felt my gumboots squelch into the mud on Papendorf's side.

I had to throw the rope across the river three times before Ivor caught it. He knew I was laughing at him. When he finally swung over, he curled his knees up like a spider to save his dance shoes from the water.

I don't know why. They were already ruined.

Chapter 9

HAS HE REACHED the surgery yet? I could check if I wanted. But the cream walls of that place still repel me. The stink of disinfectant. The shining brass plate on the front gate. Every time I used to walk down the path, I'd run my palm over the agapanthus I'd planted there.

But I can't go closer now, even though I'm trying to be strong. Not there. Not yet. Instead I'm falling. Down, down towards Plumbago Way again, where a small smudge at the bottom of the hill is thickening into a solid figure, moving at a steady pace.

Up the driveway of number twenty-two shuffles Bart. Then he lumbers down to the back fence. Panting, he leans on the top rung of the fence to bend into a stretch. His curly dark hair is matted with sweat. The fence, already bowed down with plumbago, shudders along its length, nodding its leaves as if to remind me of something I've been grasping for. Not happiness, you understand. Nothing as flimsy as that.

No, not happiness. Perhaps you could call it relief. Bart here, looking after Marianne. Princess helping out. Sylvia okay. Alwyn *more* than okay. Just the way I'd hoped it would be. Good enough. Satisfactory.

Well, of course I feel ashamed. Wouldn't anyone? Shame lurks in the pockets of the mind (or spirit), like lint. No matter how brave a face you put on things – and believe me, I did – you always have to face yourself in the end. And maybe that was the whole problem: I never wanted to face myself. I just kept putting it off again and again, until it was too late. By then everyone could see what was happening with me and there was no going back.

When you fall pregnant you can't *not* decide one way or the other what to do.

Bart made it easier, I'll admit that. The decision-making. He was always a good listener, and he seemed to understand about my not wanting to be more than friends, even though I'd clearly broken that rule once already. He also tended to forget about the bad things I'd said or done once they were over. Whereas I always took a very long time.

It happened like this: the whole town was in a palaver about Ivor and Janice's wedding. The day before, you couldn't go outside without hearing labourers banging in posts for the tarpaulin in Ivor's back yard, or florists' vans pulling up, or guests from out of town parking their Mercs and bakkies outside the Royal Hotel on Main Road.

Sylvia wasn't involved with the wedding, but she was always off somewhere, more often than not with Sandile Sinto. Most of the time I had the house to myself, and that day before the wedding was no different. Obviously, I didn't feel like going outside, so I shut myself in my bedroom with a pile of Maggie Shepherd's books.

But I couldn't concentrate on anything for long. I picked up and put down a couple of American novels and art books, but in the end I settled for a dog-eared Agatha Christie. Even then my mind kept wandering off, and I hadn't worked out who the murderer was by the fifth chapter, something I usually prided myself on. So when the doorbell rang and rang and kept on for at least ten minutes, with a couple of short breaks in between, I finally gave up and answered it.

Bart loomed over me in the doorway. For some reason our front doorbell was very low and he had to stoop to press it.

"What are your plans for tomorrow?" he asked.

"Nothing much." I kept my hand firmly on the door handle.

Bart leaned one arm up on the lintel.

"How about coming to the beach with me?" he asked. "I thought I'd test-drive my new Peugeot."

Well I knew *that* was a lie, for starters. I'd seen Bart's car parked outside the pub, and one glance was enough to tell you it was the kind of car driven by someone who didn't give a toss. Within a week that Peugeot would be cluttered with Coke tins and empty chip packets.

"No thanks," I said.

"Why?"

"*Why?* Because I don't feel like it."

"Come on, Connie." Bart scratched at the tangled black hair on his crown. His chubby face scrunched up. "Why do you always have to make things so difficult for yourself?"

"I'm not making things difficult for myself. I don't *like* going to the beach."

"Why not?"

"Because it's *boring*, that's why!" I noticed I had my hands on my hips. "Since when have you been so interested in going to the beach, anyway? Don't you have a wedding to go to?"

"I hate weddings," said Bart.

"Have you told them you're not going?" I asked. I couldn't help adding: "She gets very upset about that kind of thing, you know."

"My aunt in East London's having an emergency op," Bart said. "I have to visit her in ICU."

"Nothing serious, I hope?"

"Depends on the weather." He squinted up at the sky. "If it's sunny tomorrow it might be very serious indeed. She may take a turn for the worse. I may have to stay till she pulls through. Till around ten p.m., maybe."

He waited.

"I'm really sorry, Bart," I said, "but I'm not in the mood for visiting your sick auntie or going to the beach. Thanks for asking, though." I reached for the door handle again. I waited for him to go, but instead he put his hands on his hips and stuck out his jaw. He glared down at me. His shorts were starting to slip down from under his paunch in the time-honoured Scheepersdorp way, and even though it was still pretty chilly in the afternoons, he had a pair of slip-slops on that did nothing for his pudgy toes.

"Suit yourself," he said eventually. "Personally, I think you're just cutting off your nose to spite your face. But it's your call." He turned and shambled down the front steps to the new Peugeot parked at the bottom of my front drive, engine still running.

I shut the front door and marched back to my room. For fifteen minutes I lay on my bed reading the same sentence of *Murder at the Vicarage* over and over again. Then I got up and went to the phone in the kitchen.

I must have waited at least five minutes for Bart to come to the phone after they'd called him. I could hear people talking and glasses clinking, and some guy who kept calling for a double Klippies and Coke. Finally someone picked up the receiver.

"Bart Mayford speaking."

I said, "It's me."

"Hi." His voice was cool.

"I'm sorry I was rude to you."

"You were bloody rude. But it's okay."

"Sorry," I said again. "Thanks for asking. It was nice of you."

"Offer still stands," Bart said.

I knew if I hesitated, that would be it.

"Okay," I said to him. "Thanks. What time do you want to pick me up?"

"What about that Mayford guy, now?" Harry asked next morning. "Bart. Why don't you give that poor bastard a chance? He's no oil painting, I know. But can you afford to be fussy? Ask yourself that."

And when I didn't reply: "Listen to me, Constance. I know you're not going to listen, but *listen*. The guy's got a good job. He earns a decent living. And man," – Harry stopped to snap a switch from the plumbago hedge – "have you ever tasted one of those Hunger-Buster burgers they make down there at his restaurant? That guy knows how to cook!"

It was early on the morning of Ivor and Janice's wedding, and I was dragging myself behind Harry through his orchard. At half past five he'd banged on my bedroom window to wake me. When I didn't get up quickly enough, he took the spare key out of the flower pot and sent Soapy scrabbling in through the kitchen door. I could hear her panting long before she got to me, and when she reached my room she collapsed from the effort, right on top of the jeans I'd thrown off when I fell into bed the night before. They were covered in blackjacks and still smelled of buchu.

Soapy should have been home in her basket. It took all her energy just to get outside a few times a day. But she was like Harry: she never wanted to miss out on anything.

I didn't mind. I'd been awake since four. If I'd slept three hours that night it was a lot.

When I eventually stumbled out onto the stoep, pulling on

my socks and boots, Harry was waiting with a mug of coffee and a couple of Letty's rusks.

"Jeez. You look like something the cat's dragged in."

He didn't know my kit-bag was ready at the back door, packed with my towel and swimming cozzie for when Bart came to fetch me at seven.

"I think you should get out of town for a while. Take a holiday," Harry said as I trailed after him across the plot.

The mist was dissolving and there wasn't a cloud in the blue, blank sky above the Kanonkop. It was going to be a beautiful day. Perfect for a wedding.

"I don't want to talk about it," I said. "Anyway, I can't leave the nursery."

"Man – *I'll* look after the nursery for you. Or we'll get that lazy bastard Alwyn to shift his arse into gear."

"Why should I get out of town?" I said as Harry pushed open his back gate and I followed him into the orchard. "I live here too, you know. In fact, I was here first."

"Jesus, Constance."

"Everybody seems to think I should be making things easier for them. What about *me*?"

"Taste here." Harry snatched at a tree and shoved a plum at me. "You won't get fruit like *this* at Naidoo's Fruiterers." Then: "Never get between husband and wife."

"How can you even *think* I'd try to do that?" I batted his hand away.

"Do what?"

"Break Janice and Ivor up."

"Did I say that? I never said that. You're not listening."

"What *are* you saying then?"

"I'm just saying – that Janice is a very nice woman, hey? Always smiling. *You* could learn a lot from her."

64

"What does *that* mean?"

"Don't get uptight, now." Harry pushed the plum at me again. "Taste."

"Can you not understand that I don't want to talk about Janice, today of all days?"

"You're too intense!" Harry rammed the plum in my mouth. "Go on," he yelled, "tell me that's not the sweetest plum you're gonna get! I'm trying to *help* you, is all," he continued, ignoring my choking. "If *I* don't tell you these things, who will? Those two," – flinging an arm at Ivor and Janice's place – "are starting off their married life today. And they sure as hell don't need *you* messing things up, Constance West. Walking round with that look on your face like you got rotten fish under your nose."

"Thanks." I managed to swallow a mouthful of plum and spit the pip out.

"Oh, Jesus. You're taking it personally."

"What you're saying is incredibly hurtful to me."

"You're too sensitive! *That's* your problem. You need to toughen up! Life isn't for sissies, you know. You gotta roll with the punches. Look at Janice now." Harry cracked a pecan with his teeth. "She hasn't had it all her way. But she puts a good face on things. She's got a bubbly kind of personality, you know? People *like* her—" Harry turned and saw my face. His arms dropped to his sides. "Oh no. Don't cry, Connie, I hate it when you cry. I just—" Pressing his thumbs into his eyes. "God, this is giving me such a headache. I just *care* about you, is all. Constance, I'm only trying to help."

As I flung open the orchard gate and belted across the plot for home, Harry's voice boomeranged after me across the Kanonkop valley: "Would you rather I didn't *care*?"

There was just enough time for me to scrub my face and comb my hair before Bart came to pick me up.

* * *

The wedding ceremony was at four o'clock at the Anglican Church on Main Road. The reception was at Ivor's house at six, so I guessed the party would carry on until at least three a.m.

It's a good two-hour drive from Scheepersdorp to the nearest beach. That's if you use the shortcut. So when Bart picked me up and took the long way round, all through the dirt roads via Peddie and Berlin, I didn't say anything. We both knew he'd worked out a way to keep us out of Scheepersdorp as long as possible.

We had fun testing all the gadgets in the new Peugeot: cruise control, seat-belt reminder, surround sound.

"All we need now," I told Bart on the way home, "is to have an accident. Then we can test the airbags too."

But we didn't.

Well.

Not *that* kind of accident.

Afterwards, I tried explaining it to him: it wasn't him. It was the day out and the smell of new leather and the feeling of my skin being tanned and salty that put it all together. I told him he shouldn't count on it happening again.

I truly believed I was being honest with him. There was nothing about him I considered sexy. I've never found big men attractive, and Bart towered over me. Tall, but also carrying at least ten kilos more than he should. His pale skin freckled in the Scheepersdorp summer. His curly black hair straggled out like a weed, no matter how often it got cut, and he kept running his tubby fingers through it to keep it out of his eyes. To make things worse, it was thinning on the crown.

But he *did* have a way of keeping quiet when I talked to him. Not in a way that made me think he was bored. More like he was concentrating on every word I said. It scared me a little.

That night, on the way home, I started talking. I told him stuff I hadn't even told Sylvia. Through the windscreen, the moon blurred in the mist as the car whipped along. I talked and talked and Bart didn't say a word. I told him about Sylvia and Alwyn and me. Climbing the Kanonkop and the things we hid under the yellowwood tree. How the three of us did everything together until Ivor came to town. Who knows? If we'd driven any further I might have ended up telling him about Ivor, too. He wouldn't have batted an eyelid – not even if I told him what I'd spent half the previous night worrying about. But just then the Scheepersdorp lights drifted into sight beyond the next hill, and Bart slowed the car. When he shifted gear his enormous hands were quite steady. Driving into Main Road, he glanced across at me and smiled. The light from a street lamp fell across his face. I'd never noticed before how blue his eyes were.

And, as I've said before, there was the smell of that new leather.

I didn't answer my door or my phone the next night. Or the next. At work, I told them to take a message, and I made sure I was on site all day.

Bart only left a message once. "Thanks for last night," he said on my answering machine. I couldn't tell if he was being sarcastic.

You can say I was imagining it, but within the space of a day I'd already started to feel sick. I couldn't face drinking coffee. And when I started passing on the tea-time doughnuts at work, there were a few strange glances my way.

Princess couldn't believe it when she made bobotie on Monday and it was still untouched in the fridge by Wednesday. Friday she found me retching into the toilet bowl.

"Ohhh Connie." She splayed a skinny hand over her mouth. "Sorry, sorry. Maybe you eat something bad?"

I shook my head and told her I'd be okay. When Bart came by later I didn't answer the door.

I *told* him, I hummed to myself while I waited in the dark kitchen for him to go away. I held Jakkals on my lap, muzzling her snout with one hand. I *told* him it wouldn't happen again.

Chapter 10

"How am I supposed to get anywhere," I ask, "when I don't know who to follow? It's half past eleven already and I still don't know why I'm here." I'm aware a whining note has crept into my voice.

The Boatman appears not to have heard. He's leaning both elbows on the peeling green paint of the iron railing above the Kangela River, almost shoulder to shoulder with Alwyn. And Alwyn is wedged close to Princess, splendid in her church uniform. Her polished black court shoes, which once belonged to me, are planted neatly on the pavement beside Alwyn's size-twelve veldskoens. I'd only worn them once, for Harry Healey's last mayoral induction. Lucky for Princess we were the same size. For a full five minutes, the three of them have been staring down at the water below, rolling heavy and fast.

The peace that passeth all understanding – there was certainly a time I yearned for that. And I'm not sure I feel any different now. What a mess. These people. Their dramas and decisions. What do they have to do with me?

As if he's read my thoughts, the Boatman turns to consider me. One second he's in a lab coat, with a stethoscope. Then he's a young boy, crouched over a desk, buttoned into a white shirt and khaki shorts. You can tell it's him from the shape of those eyes. That and the disproportionately small hands, looping letters into an exercise book. Then he's back in a three-piece suit, slapping a copy of *Business Day* against his thigh.

"What's your name?" I blurt. He seems less surprised than I am that I've finally had the nerve to ask.

Just when I think he's not going to reply, he says, "Mkhaliphi. Dr Dingikhaya Mkhaliphi."

The stain across his chest is back, pulsing darker and stickier now, and I resist the impulse to reach forward and touch it.

"Why are *you* here?" I ask.

From the corners of his eyes, Dr Mkhaliphi glances at Princess and Alwyn making their way from the bridge towards the path down to the river. But he doesn't turn away from me.

"*I* think," he meets my gaze again, "you need to be brave now, Ms West."

He stares down at me, and his dark pupils glint like rocks under a black river. For the first time I feel I've been given some kind of clue.

Perhaps he thought me a coward, too. Ivor. Perhaps he thought it was my being too scared to look at what was happening that messed things up in the first place.

He should've known me better than that.

Courage? I'll tell you what that means. Courage is coming back here, now. To these rooms. It's those times I was left alone with the smell of Savlon and the certificates on the wall and whispered phone conversations going on in the next room.

Courage was me sliding my fingers across a desk one day to open this thick yellow file with my name on it. The very same file that's lying on the desk he's sitting at now. He's turned to stare out of the window at the smoke climbing up from Sandile Sinto's back yard, and his index finger's tapping at the yellow cardboard in time to the beat.

He wasn't the one who put together that file. It was his partner, Grant Rebus. I made sure of that right from the start. It was Grant I went to see first, and Grant who referred me to the doctor in PE. After she spelt it all out for me, I told Grant I didn't want Ivor involved. Between Grant and the specialist, my treatment could be managed from Scheepersdorp. Being practical about things like that made me feel more in control.

Though reading that file, I still remember, felt like having acid poured into my eyes, trickling down to my heart and lungs.

I remember thinking: they cut some parts of you away. They poison the rest. So then where's the part of you that's pure *you*? The bit, if they cut it away, that will make you no longer who you were? The person they call Connie West. Or Ivor Shepherd. The part other people recognise, and love. Or hate.

I wasn't too afraid to read that file. In time, I wasn't too scared to think about what it meant, even at two a.m. with Bart snoring healthily in the room next door, Sylvia sleeping across the passageway.

And I'm afraid, but not *too* afraid now, to finally go closer and take him in.

What's changed in the last year? Not much. When he was fifteen, a streak of white hair started growing in Ivor's fringe. Now, at thirty, the streak has broadened: there's more white than light brown. His face is fuller and there are signs of a paunch beginning to appear in that taut body. He stopped smoking two years ago – Janice saw to that – but the lines above his lips are still there, perhaps a fraction sharper. The two grooves running from nose to mouth are deeper, too. Though that could be because he's frowning as he looks down.

I never admitted how frightened I felt when he scowled at me like that.

But he's still neatly held together. Still the same compact, controlled body packed into the chair. And I'll guarantee it's still the same whirring mind shifting gear behind that unruffled face. Though I'm not drawn into that spinning centre any more. Not like I once was.

To get to the top of the Kanonkop you scramble past a Sutherlandia bush growing between two boulders. Duck left, turn right and you're there: a plateau three metres wide and about four long, stretched under the shadow of a big red rock.

"Great view," Ivor grunted the first day Alwyn and I took him up there. The air was pulled tight as cling film. It was a week after the standard-eight dance and the night I'd dared him to swing across the river.

When you're up there, Scheepersdorp lies plated beneath you: the smoke from the chimneys, the diminutive cars and houses. Their sounds are torn into confetti that drifts up to where you stand. Below, and on the hills opposite, the aloes tumble down towards the valley as if they'd been chased by a god and petrified mid-flight.

"What are you smiling at?" Ivor lit a cigarette as he prowled around the rocky perimeter. His mother didn't seem to mind when he stole her smokes. He stopped beside me to peer over the edge as if he were staring down a microscope. Behind us, Alwyn was already getting stuck into the picnic I'd brought along.

"The way you said that." I lay on my stomach, resting my chin on my hands. "'Great view. Magnificent.' You sound so British."

Alwyn looked up from the picnic, wide-eyed. He was still afraid of Ivor and his cleverness. Before Ivor, nobody at Scheepersdorp High School had ever got 100 per cent in a maths test.

There's more than one way to be clever, Alwyn, I used to tell him.

"I am British. Partly." Ivor squatted beside me, arms on his knees to stare down at Scheepersdorp. A queue was forming outside the Standard Bank on Main Road, and Princess was hanging out the washing in our back yard. Beside the crumbling river bank, a flock of hadedahs combed for grubs, their shadows blank and thick. "I don't always understand you," Ivor said.

"Why must you?"

"I'm not sure." He watched Letty Healey calling Harry in for tea from her back door. The sun glinted on the muzzle of Harry's rifle. *Pop pop pop,* the shots filtered up towards us, and the parrots exploded from the pecan-nut tree. "I don't understand many people in this town. I don't really want to."

Ivor turned to look at me. His eyes were half shut, so I couldn't quite tell what he was thinking. "Except for you," he said. "You're the only one I want to understand, Constance West."

I never once heard him shout her name like he used to yell mine. Cupping his hands from the kitchen door so his voice bounced across the Kanonkop hills and everyone knew Ivor Shepherd was calling Connie West again and he didn't give a shit who heard.

When Ivor wanted Janice he'd come shambling out to find her, like a dog sniffing for its owner. That first winter I watched them from my dark kitchen, my breath dissolving in the cold: Janice in the back garden, ideas massing around her like storm clouds. Ivor ambling over to put a hand on her shoulder. The smoke piling up out of the fireplace at number fourteen. A signal to the whole of Scheepersdorp.

The old Shepherd house trembled with life. Windows were opened. Doors flung wide. She stood in the back yard, where I'd scattered vygies and bobbejaantjies from the Kop, sweeping her arm wide as she talked. Her other arm was around Ivor.

Make a space over there, she told me a week later. *Connie, that's going to be the trampoline. Leave some room for a jungle gym. I want one with a slide.*

This is so perfect, she said. *You living right next door.*

That was before someone finally took pity on her and told her.

Is that why I'm here? Fine. I forgive him. It's not that difficult.

Let bygones be bygones, Harry always said. Or Alwyn: *Connie. You have buttered your bread. Now you must lie on it.*

It doesn't hurt to see Ivor, not like it used to. Hopefully I'm beyond hurt and irritation now. Maybe it's plain curiosity pulling me in. If I've only got till sunset, I may as well go with that.

If I could, I might even be willing to warn him that this very minute someone's kapping down Bloubessie Way towards his surgery. Fully focused as only she can be, her long shadow rippling ahead of her, her slim feet in white summer sandals: Janice is on a mission to fetch him home.

He doesn't need any warning from me. He's got more than enough time between the squeaking of the gate and the opening of the surgery door to push the file back into the bottom drawer and lock it shut. But he doesn't.

Most people in Scheepersdorp preferred Janice to me. To be sure, she scared them all a bit, with her legal know-how and her Gucci sunglasses. But she was so *nice* about everything. So ready to share. She knew how to work a video machine. She told everyone about the boutique in PE where she bought her linen suits and blouses. She kept a weekly appointment with Elle Chic salon so her ginger bob (was that colour *really* natural?) never deviated from its even bounce. And she was so *interested* in all of us. Most of all, she'd managed to get through to Ivor like nobody else. People fell in love with her instantly.

Even now, grinning at him from around the door, fresh

highlights in her bob, a light powdering of blusher, Janice knows better than to ask why he hasn't answered his phone all morning. What he's doing hanging round the empty surgery so long after closing hours.

You can bet she's taken in the yellow file on the desk, and the name written on the front. But she knows better than to ask about that, too.

She knows when the time is right she'll discover what it all means. Janice is a great believer in timing. Like now, for instance. They need to get home soon.

Chapter 11

PEOPLE ARE STREAMING towards the bridge at the bottom of town. From the taxi rank they pour through Scheepersdorp Square past the statue of Queen Victoria. The child with the gumboots; the man with my old garden hat. A woman selling herbs on the pavement bundles them up, tucks them under her arm and trots towards Bridge Road. Fat and disapproving, Victoria frowns down at them all.

One woman starts to ululate. Another joins in. Then another. Above the *doef-doef* of taxi music, their voices vibrate. Soon the sound is echoing against the Kanonkop hills: *Rie-rie-rie-rierierieeeee*.

From the front stoep of number twenty-two Plumbago Way, Bart leans out to look towards town, shading his eyes. Less than twenty metres away, Esmé, too, has come down to her front fence. Hands folded beneath her apron, she peers in the same direction.

Aiyeeeee-eee-eee. The shrieks sweep up Plumbago Way.

Within seconds, Esmé's front door has slammed shut. The key twists in the lock. The bolt slides across and the chain rattles into place.

Since last year's elections, Esmé has kept a larder in her garage fully stocked with tins and dry goods. Plus a small generator and a fifteen-litre can of diesel. On the table in her lounge is a Flip File of letters and faxes warning what will happen once majority rule is established in Scheepersdorp. There is also advice about what to do in a power failure and how to purify contaminated water.

Some people have mocked her for this. Esmé presses her thin lips together, victorious. Who's sorry now? Through the firmly shut windows of her lounge, a chorus of faint, trembling cries still manages to slip through.

Two houses away, Harry Healey is about to push the block of stinkwood through the lathe yet again when he stops to listen. Whatever else has changed, his ears are as sharp as always. Harry flicks the machine off. Block of wood in one hand, he strides down the front yard and onto the tar of Plumbago Way. Sawdust has powdered his hair to a soft blond, and the denim apron Letty sewed for him is tied loosely at the back. In the gap between tee-shirt and shorts a healthy plumber's crack shows exactly what Harry thinks of them all: neighbours, disobedient women, Scheepersdorp.

Sylvia's washing glasses in the kitchen when Sandile dashes in, the rotting floorboards bouncing them both gently up and down.

"You have to see this." He pulls her from the sink, down the dark passageway and out of the front door. Sylvia barely has time to dry her hands.

"What's happening?" she cries, but already they're jogging across the slasto path towards the BMW parked in the driveway. Sandile nods at the iron gates and Sylvia scuttles to open them, closing them behind the car again before hopping into the passenger seat.

There was a time Sandile would have sprinted the five hundred metres from his house to the bridge. He might even have got there in less time than it took to drive through the traffic and potholes. Not any more. Sandile snaps his seatbelt on. The BMW shifts into gear and turns right, then right again, gunning down Bloubessie Way, taking a sharp left into Main Road.

People, people everywhere. Sandile eases past taxis and cars, through the masses milling towards the road out of town. Just short of the bridge, he pulls over and parks in the loading zone next to the brand-new Kentucky Fried. Almost before he's braked, he and Sylvia leap out, barely remembering to lock the car before darting past the abandoned taxi in the middle of the road. Dragging Sylvia behind him, Sandile fights his way through the crowd to the railing.

Below, two figures are picking their way down the river bank towards the water's edge, one in red-and-white church uniform, the other in blue denims and a tee with a towel round his neck.

The rains have been good this year. Eighteen months ago, there were only rocks and Coke cans and Pick n Pay bags scattered on the dry river bed. Now the malt-coloured water is foaming at the rocks. It shoulders the river banks aside as if something urgent is calling it to sea. If it goes on like this, there'll be floods, though at the moment it's still possible for an adult to wade across.

Under a bush on the left bank, a pair of denims, a tee-shirt, size-twelve veldskoens and a towel have been neatly folded. Parked on the right bank are my two polished black shoes, side by side, as if someone's taken them off before getting into bed.

Somebody has placed a beam of wood across the rocks, forming a gangplank to a huge boulder in the middle of the river. That's where Princess is standing now, arms spread wide. A starched, brilliant-white lab coat, which can only have come from Harry, is buttoned over her church clothes. Princess has rolled the sleeves back at least three times, and the hem drops well beyond her feet down to the rock; the fabric's already darkened with water. Her bare toes cling to the flat edge of the rock, and in one hand she holds a stick carved from stinkwood.

You can hardly hear a thing over the women ululating and the kwaito music from the minibus and the rush of water. But the tune Princess is humming rises above it, clear and somehow familiar to me, though I can't think from where.

She's a sly one, that's for sure. So unctuous and obedient when she needed to be: *Yes Connie. No Connie. Oohhh Connie, sorry sorry sorry*, hand over mouth, watching from the bathroom doorway as I chucked it all up for the third day in a row.

Look at her. Waves are lapping at her toes, but she keeps steady on the uneven rock. She even sways as she hums, eyes shut.

From the bridge, Sandile leans over for a better view. He nudges Sylvia and points to the river bank on the other side. Sylvia cranes her neck to see.

Stripped down to purple board shorts, Alwyn is making his way towards the rock where Princess waits. His elbows pump sideways, chest-height, as he half-jogs, half-wades through the water. Nothing can stop him now. Not the crowd on the river banks, not the taxis' booming music nor the women ululating. Not even Princess's low, humming moan that almost takes on the urgency of the river. Nothing can stop Alwyn van der Walt. Certainly not me.

Not that I'd want to. I mean: I know that look. That obsessive, green-eyed, take-no-prisoners intensity. Just like when we were small and he learned how to shoot a catty, even better than Sandile. Just like he used to latch himself on to things and never let them go. And people. His mother. Sylvia. Bart. Me.

He's only a metre from Princess now, sliding his big feet carefully over rocks and shingle and water-smoothed pieces of glass. By the time he reaches her, the water's churning creamy yellow around his belly.

Only when he finally drops his elbows, ducks, then pushes his hands onto the rock to hoist himself up can you see it properly: the thick scar running down the centre of his chest. Water droplets dribble right off the pink, twisted tissue.

Rising on tiptoes, Princess ignores him as she stretches her arms wider and starts to sing. At her feet Alwyn hunches, gasping, water puddling around his thighs.

By now, some of the crowd have spilled down to the river bank. Among them is the Boatman. He's standing right in front, ankle-deep in water, trousers rolled up and shoes in one hand. How worn out he looks. As he opens his mouth to sing, his reddened eyes wander to where I stand at my sister's side. His baritone glides into the sea of voices like a fish released.

Kukho umlambo omisinga isivuyisayo isixeko sikaThixo, esilikhaya elingcwele …

"What are they singing?" Sylvia asks. Like me, she has only a smattering of Xhosa. But Sandile's lips are already curving into the next verse.

I didn't ask to come back and see this. Any more than I asked to suddenly understand these clicking, twitching sounds. They always seemed so impenetrable to me. Like a thorny kraal keeping me out. How is it, now, that they are disintegrating into pure meaning? The Boatman winks at me.

There is a river, the streams whereof shall make glad the city of God, the holy place … The Boatman sways from side to side.

Dala phakathi kwam, Thixo, intliziyo ehlambulukileyo, the crowd sings. *Uhlaziye umoya oqinisekileyo phakathi kwam.*

Create in me a clean heart, O God; renew a right spirit within me.

Dala phakathi kwam. Thixo. Princess's voice spirals into the chorus again. Eighty or more voices avalanche after hers. Eighty pairs of hands clap, marking the beat. Princess tucks her elbows in and manages a shuffling jig at the front of the rock. Finally she holds up her arms for silence.

When the last note rolls to a halt, Princess lowers her arms. On cue, Alwyn slides back into the river, the water rising to his shoulders. Princess leans down to mutter in his ear. Then she lays her stick on the rock and pushes aside the thick lab coat to lower herself to her knees, almost face to face with Alwyn. She lifts her arms once more, fingers spread, as if showing us all she has nothing to hide. For a moment, she rests them on Alwyn's spiked crown. Then she presses down, hard. Once. Twice. Three times she ducks him under the water.

In the sudden hush, Dr Mkhaliphi drops his head back and shuts his eyes. Hands behind his back, he rocks lightly on his toes.

High above them all, in the thinnest current of air, a falcon spirals over Scheepersdorp. If anyone from the river bank looked up, it would seem to them like a dust mote gliding in the air. To the soaring bird, the people below look like tiny islands pulling together and drawing apart. The metallic blink of the river as one figure steps back on the rock. The other lies back in the water. The wiry-thin scribbles of sound twine up through the air.

That song Princess is humming. It's not the psalm the crowd was singing a few minutes ago. It's that other tune, the one I know from somewhere … *Ndiza kukuncedisa ukugoduka* … It drags me in and flings me out again. Every time I try to get closer, she sings louder and rolls her eyes back.

Arms spread at right-angles to his scarred chest, Alwyn lies in the river, his huge feet dipping and rising in the current. He shuts his eyes against the sun, shattered into a billion pieces on the water.

Dala phakathi kwam, Thixo. The crowd sings on.

Ndiza kukuncedisa ukugoduka. Princess croons the other, strange tune under the thundering hymn. Together they drown out the noise of the traffic and the beat of the taxi music and even the harsh, almost human cries of the hadedahs pulling towards the top of the Kanonkop. It simply is, and I stay well away.

Princess used to sing while she was working – all the time, till it nearly drove me bloody nuts. I'd shut the kitchen door on her pointedly. If that didn't work, I'd stomp down the passage and slam my bedroom door to get the message through. But it never sank in. She'd just carry on crooning away, pushing the mop or the iron to and fro like she was in a trance.

Once, when I'd given her a blurt about coming to work late again, she told me that where she grew up, they used to tell the time by how long the shadows stretched from the cattle horns in the morning.

All good and well, I told her, *but I've got a watch. And so have you.*

All I wanted when I got home from work each day was a bit of peace and quiet. But she'd be tuned in to Radio Xhosa, full blast. Some daily serial where they were always shouting at each other. Or crying.

Please, Princess, I told her, *I get enough of that from the neighbours. You're going to have to turn it down.*

She'd get that blank expression on her face. Then, finger by finger, she'd wipe her hands on a paper serviette, reach for the dial and turn it right off.

It didn't matter. Next day we'd be back to normal again. That means, within five minutes of Sylvia making coffee in the kitchen, or Alwyn coming over for a beer, Princess would appear miraculously from wherever she'd been working – usually way at the other end of the house – and pull out the ironing board.

Without a word she'd bring out the basket of clean washing and start ironing. Absolutely no shame. While Sylvia and I talked, Princess would press and fold, iron and spray, sometimes humming under her breath. No wonder news in Scheepersdorp spread faster than the common cold.

She thought I didn't notice her ironing the same shirt over and over again the day Sylvia came in to tell me about Janice and Ivor's wedding plans.

Sorrysorrysorry, Princess said six months later when she found me retching over the toilet bowl, *Oh sorry, Con*. When she said my name it sounded like "Corn".

But she never asked, even when it became more and more obvious.

Oh my God, she screamed when I walked into the kitchen and eventually told her what she'd already known for ages. She had her hands in the sink but she grabbed me in her skinny arms and lifted me right off my feet, slathering hot soapy water down my back.

Oh Connie, God is good to you, she warbled. *We going to hope it going to be the girl.*

The girls they look after the mamas, Con, she said when she finally put me down again.

I didn't take much notice. I didn't much care what she thought. But one thing I was glad about: she was the only one who never asked me about the father.

"What now?" I sighed. Because I was getting more and more pissed off, I can tell you, with my old friend Alwyn and his non-stop laziness. A windgat. That's what he was becoming. Moan, moan, moan all day long and nothing to show for it.

I was rummaging around in Esmé's baking cupboard because I craved something sweet, but also so I didn't have to pretend to be serious with that Eeyore face staring up at me.

But when I turned round to dunk the rusk in the lousy, weak Ricoffy he'd struggled to make, I noticed his breathing again.

Hsrrhgh harrrh, like a broom sweeping across a tiled floor. His face was white as the porcelain coffee mug he'd set in front of me, and his lips were tinted purplish blue.

He said, "I'm serious, Con," then stopped to draw breath again. "Ivor says I must see a specialist."

"What specialist?" I stood at the table dunking my rusk. I didn't want him to see how spooked I really was.

In any case, why should he get more sympathy than I did? Life was just one shitty thing after another, and I wasn't complaining, was I? I didn't go round asking everyone to feel sorry for me.

Can't you ever think anything will turn out right, Con? Alwyn asked once. *Don't you believe there's something you can do about things?* He asked it the same way a child would. He wasn't saying it to get at me. And for once I saw that, so I didn't have a go at him.

Sylvia said, *You can't control what happens to you. But you can control your reaction to it.*

In other words, Con, Ivor whispered in my ear, *if life hands you lemons, you make ginger ale.*

Esmé was in the kitchen with Alwyn and me that day, but she didn't say a word. Just carried on scrubbing the kitchen floor, grinding her teeth behind that flabby jaw of hers. You'd think she'd wear that floor down to paper the way she went at it. I even saw her get a toothpick to clean the groove between the zinc basin and the counter.

"Groote Schuur Hospital," Alwyn told me. "Ivor wants to send me to Cape Town for an investiment by the specialist."

"You mean assessment." I pulled out one of Esmé's Formica chairs and sat down. My back was starting to hurt.

"Look at me," I said. But he kept staring down at his hands and fiddling with them like they were some kind of Chinese puzzle.

"Alwyn. Man."

84

But his head stayed bowed.

"They have ways to fix these things," I said. "You can trust Ivor, you know. He knows about these things. He knows the right people." I went on: "You've got to look after yourself, for your mom's sake. For all our sakes. You moegoe." I prodded his arm. "I need you to help *me* now."

I looked over my shoulder as I said it, speaking under my breath to make sure Esmé didn't hear. Besides Bart, Alwyn was the only one I'd told so far. Fortunately I wasn't showing that much, especially when I wore one of the baggy knitted jerseys I'd stolen from Sylvia's cupboard.

Finally he lifted his head. His eyes wavered at me, a muddy olive shade. "There's Bart," he muttered.

"Bart's not you," I whispered back, "and I've chosen you to be godfather. We both have. God knows," – I glanced over my shoulder again and leaned forward – "if any child needs spiritual help it's going to be this one. So you have to do the best you can. Go lie down, and for God's sake take your bladdy rest for once without everyone having a moan about it. You can have a decent break now, for free." And I slapped him on the knee, a bit too hard perhaps. "How difficult is that?"

Chapter 12

IN THE OLD DAYS – by that I mean the days before Janice came to Scheepersdorp – Ivor would lock his room at the surgery at one and eat a sandwich behind his desk. Sometimes he'd park himself on the wooden bench at the bottom of the surgery garden, hidden behind a mirror bush so no one could see him and try to strike up a conversation.

People weren't so different to plants, he told me once. Diseases; companionship; the right amount of distance in a relationship. Their genus determined their ills. A vigorous, healthy plant did not invite illness, he'd say, lighting up a post-sandwich Stuyvesant.

He never asked where I'd been, never pestered me about what was I thinking or where was I going, like Bart would do in time. I thought Ivor liked it that way. I thought that was the right distance for him and me. Perhaps I should have paid more attention. Maybe I would have worked it out then. Or he might have bothered to tell me, if he thought I'd listen. Maybe he wasn't that different from other people, after all.

Today there will be no sandwiches in the surgery garden for lunch. Three blocks away, in the home Janice has made in Maggie Shepherd's house, lunch has been prepared. There is home-baked bread, and two bowls of carrot salad, and slivers of beef so thin you can see through them to the blue Noritake plate on which they lie in overlapping circles.

Carpaccio, Janice calls them. And though she dithered about it long enough, she eventually decided she *would* set out a table in the back garden, facing the roses and the willow tree and the tall fence with the wild plot beyond. Just for good luck, just for courage, and because she has tried so *very* hard, she treated herself to a small G and T there before leaving to fetch Ivor from the surgery. At this stage, a half-tot will do more good than harm.

Even though Janice is eager to leave, to get back home to the beef carpaccio and the home-baked bread, the Gordon's gin and, most importantly, the enormous feather bed ordered from PE, she and Ivor have still not left the surgery.

For five minutes now she's been pottering around his consulting room, picking things up, putting them down again. Only a light spattering of freckles has managed to settle on that milky skin, something you'd think might highlight her frailty and elegance. Except that, rather than swaying gracefully, her long limbs teeter from object to object. Janice picks up the plastic replica of a cross-sectioned heart. She turns it over in her palm, seemingly engrossed. She has learned very quickly that when Ivor casts that cold wall around himself, she has to tread with care.

She lifts the framed head-and-shoulders shot of herself and Ivor, their hair iced with confetti. Two years ago, the bells of St Andrew's vibrated through the afternoon shoppers on Scheepersdorp Square. The mist pulled back from the valley, and when she and Ivor walked down the stone steps of the church, married, a minibus taxi hurtled past, thudding with music. The driver hooted and the passengers ululated and waved. Merrily, merrily she began her married life. So Sylvia told me afterwards.

Kinders by dosyne / Teel hul soos konyne, Alwyn and his friends

87

sang at the reception at Ivor's rose-ringed house. Even Ivor cracked a smile.

"Why she can't make the babies, Con?" Princess asked almost a year later.

We were talking about the generous salary offer Janice had made Princess to come and work for her.

"Oh, Connie." Princess shook her head. "I tell her – I can't do this, Janice. I tell her: is the baby. I not going to leave Connie and no one going to help her with that baby." Marianne was four weeks old by then. "I tell her: When you have the babies, Janice," – as usual, Princess was eager to fill me in on *everything* – "maybe I come look after them for you, too."

"God, Princess. You *mustn't* say that. She doesn't like people talking about that."

But when could we ever stop people from skindering about us? Or thinking private thoughts? Princess picked up one of Marianne's pink Babygros and pressed down on it till the ironing board creaked. Neither of us was going to discuss the real reason she wouldn't leave me to work for Janice. Not yet.

"Can we go now?" Janice knows this is not the best way to approach things, but her patience has finally worn thin. "We've got three hours. I took my temperature just now, and we need to do it soon."

Ivor finally stirs. He's still sitting upright behind the desk, but now he turns his head slowly to look at his wife. Silhouetted against the window in her summer blouse and skirt, Janice towers above him, smiling.

"I feel like a fucking *machine*," Ivor growls. All the same, he pushes back his chair to stand. He reaches for the jacket behind the door.

"You're *my* fucking machine." Janice tries to take his arm as they leave, but he slides out of reach.

*   *   *

"You can't teach an old cat new tricks, hey," Alwyn told Janice. She'd only been in town a couple of weeks, and he was trying to explain how things worked.

"I've lived in Scheepersdorp my whole life," he continued, "I've known Connie since the day she was born. We were pikkies together. This high," and he held his bony hand fifty centimetres off the floor. "My mom mos took Connie and Sylvia in when their mom died, hey. They lived with us till they were old enough to move back next door on their own. Me and Connie," – jamming index and middle fingers together and shooting them into the air – "we're like this. Cut me, and Connie gets a bruise."

I felt my wrist being pinched between chubby, hot fingers. Then my hand was hoisted above the cluttered table of beer bottles and wine glasses and cigarette ends. "A little experiment," giggled Bart. He lunged for a steak knife.

"I'm serious man, Bart." Alwyn was not easily put off. "One thing you got to know about this town," he banged his bottle of Castle on the counter, "is how far back people go, man. It's no good tuning someone if he's cousin or best friends with your neighbour, or the oke you work with."

Even though Toppie de Bruyn claimed Janice was the best legal mind he'd ever worked with, she still had to sip her drink in the ladies' bar at the Scheepersdorp Country Club. But down at Bart's Pub and Grill, the wind of change had begun to blow. It took Bart six months to set the place up, but he came from Joburg – that stuff was old hat to him. He reckoned Scheepersdorp was ready for a pub and steakhouse, and he was right.

At Bart's, we all sat together at the stinkwood counter curving in front of the salad bar. Janice kept her arm threaded through Ivor's. You could almost feel sorry for her, she looked so happy. It was one of the few times we all spent together before somebody told her about Ivor and me. I managed it well enough. And for

Janice, ignorance was bliss. Turning her face from me to Sylvia and back to Alwyn like we were some rare new species of ape.

"Come on, Alwyn." Janice laid a hand on his sleeve. I noticed she was always touching people. "Have you seriously never wanted to leave?"

"Never. You ask Connie." Alwyn beat the Castle bottle on the wooden counter in time to his words. "I. Have. Never. Wanted. To leave. Scheepersdorp."

"Never wanted to leave your mother, more like."

"Sis man, Con," Alwyn grinned, "I know I'm my mother's only child, but …"

"And you, Connie?" Janice swivelled back to me. "Have *you* never wanted to leave?"

Everyone waited to hear what I had to say. I leaned over to grab the bottle of pinotage and fill my glass again, and I noticed there was still dirt under my nails from the trees I'd planted that morning.

"Not really," I muttered eventually.

I looked over at Janice. Until then I hadn't realised how enchanting it was to have someone so attentive, so concerned, so … one might almost say *obsessed* with knowing you. You'll think that strange, I know, given the character I seem to be. But I couldn't help responding to her.

"Sometimes," I admitted. "Mostly I'm happy with what I've got here. I know everyone. These are the people I'm comfortable with."

Mostly.

I could see her turning that over once or twice, the thought of my uncertain comfort.

And I could see Ivor watching her. When he caught me watching him he looked away again.

Chapter 13

OVER THE KANONKOP barrels the north wind, sifting through trees, unsettling posters clinging to the street lights. One o'clock. The Saturday crowds have started to dissolve, leaving a tide of plastic bags and newspapers and cigarette butts on the streets of Scheepersdorp. On Main Road, one of the posters flies loose in the wind, flipping the serene grin of Sandile Sinto over and over in the air.

Sinto for Mayor, the caption reads. *The man for ALL the Scheepersdorp people.*

And all because Harry Healey hated waste. He hated waste and he hated people telling him what to do. In Letty's kitchen nothing was thrown away: a bin for chicken feed, a bin for compost, and a bin for the bottles and tins Harry used in his workshop.

It didn't take long, all those years ago, for Harry to notice how sharp his caddy was. Seemed a waste not to use it. Hammer, screwdriver, five iron, chipping wedge. Harry's little shadow was taught to anticipate his every need.

On summer evenings, Sandile would lug Harry's golf clubs into the back yard for chipping practice. Harry would aim over the orchard fence towards the hole and pin he'd created (with Sandile) near the river bank at the bottom of the plot. Sandile's job was to scramble down and bring the balls back again. When he found one, he'd dig his gappy front teeth into his bottom lip and give a piercing whistle, just like Harry taught him once he realised he was never going to fix that smile. In some ways, Sandile was the boy Harry would have preferred to Sylvia or me.

Sandile knew Harry better than anyone else. He knew all about the volcanic rage, the hurling of the number-five iron that refused to chip, the putter that insisted on dribbling left and so got bent in half. He was so good at understanding Harry's needs that he was soon being used for other things. On Saturday mornings he cleaned up Harry's workshop and polished his clubs before tee-off at twelve. Sunday afternoons, he came back to scale the pecan trees and sling netting over to protect them from the parrots. (Some nights he came back with his friends to bag the pecans himself.) Sandile knew the weave and bob of least resistance in dealing with Harry. He knew there would be a calm to follow the storm.

And Harry wasn't slow to see Sandile's potential. At first he toyed with the idea of sending him to Scheepersdorp Builders during the school holidays. If the kid could learn how to work a lathe and lay bricks, he'd end up pretty handy one day. And still be free to caddy on weekends.

Sandile had other ideas. When Harry talked about apprenticeship, Sandile just shook his head and stared at the ground. He let Harry rage and rail at him till there was nothing left. Every Sunday evening he'd go home to Kangela Township behind the Kop, then pitch up at Harry's place again on Monday after school as if nothing had happened. He'd clean Harry's clubs, and at five p.m. he'd tote them down to the back yard for Harry's chipping practice. All this with that smooth mask on his face, that smile it was impossible for any of us to penetrate. The days of me and Alwyn and Sylvia playing together on the river bank with him were long gone.

At the end of every term, Sandile hung around Harry's back yard with his school report. He wanted to show Harry what the teachers were saying, how well he was doing. Along with the report cards he'd bring the tattered application forms for boarding school. Then he and Harry would go through the whole loud, scripted production all over again.

Things might have gone on like that for a long time if Toppie de Bruyn hadn't given them a final push. He and some of the others at the golf club started moaning at Harry for encouraging Sandile. *The boy's getting too white*, they said. *He'll start thinking he pisses champagne.* Harry was asking for trouble. *Next thing you know*, Toppie's beady eyes swivelled at Harry, *he'll be wanting to play golf with us. They ALL will.* And it would all be Harry's fault.

Harry waited till he was sure Toppie and the others were out in their front yards one Saturday morning before he and Sandile climbed into the red bakkie. Sandile wasn't perched on the back of the truck in the time-honoured Scheepersdorp way. Harry strapped him into the passenger seat, sitting bolt upright on a couple of cushions so nobody could miss him.

Down the length of Plumbago Way and into Main Road Harry idled in second gear, looking straight ahead. Halfway down Main Road he put his indicator on and pulled off to adjust his side mirrors. For a good minute he fussed with them. Then he took a wide, slow left into the dirt road signposted *Fort Mountjoy Catholic School: 50 kilometres.*

The deal was Harry would pay for school fees if Sandile caddied for him in the holidays. Most of the time, the arrangement worked. But Scheepersdorp wouldn't have been Scheepersdorp if Harry's back door didn't crash open at least one Saturday a month, with Harry bellowing for Sandile. All the old, familiar phrases and words came spewing out: *Where The Hell. Ungrateful Bastard. That Education I Wasted On You.* When Sandile pitched up the following week as if nothing had happened, things picked up where they'd left off.

He seemed to be doing well at the school. Harry enjoyed taking Sandile's report cards down to the club to show Toppie and the others. The nuns wrote that Sandile had great potential, he was a hard worker. A born leader. Harry liked mentioning that just as Toppie was about to tee off.

When Sandile vanished shortly after writing matric, people said he'd gone to Swaziland. When we asked Princess about him, we knew by the way she shrugged her shoulders to leave the subject alone.

Letty said Sandile could at least have written to thank Harry for what he'd done. Harry yelled loud enough for the whole of Plumbago Way to hear that Sandile Sinto was too busy starting a bladdy revolution to send a Hallmark card from Swaziland. And besides. The boy owed him nothing. You understand, woman? Not a thing.

Until he popped up out of seemingly nowhere to organise the fundraiser for the Khoisan exhibition, none of us had a clue where Sandile had been or what he'd been up to. Nobody cottoned on about him and Sylvia either, though at least I suspected earlier than most.

Sandile tried to talk to me about her once. I don't know whether he was being kind, or he just felt the urge to unburden himself. "Some people don't like change, Constance," he murmured. He was folded into the armchair beside my bed, legs steepled in front of him. "Some people are very threatened by change. But it must come."

He was quiet for a long time. I was drifting in and out of listening, but I don't think he needed a response.

"Your sister," Sandile coughed. He tried again: "She's a remarkable woman, hey?"

I opened my eyes. Sandile was gazing, not at me, but out of the window, swinging his tortoiseshell glasses in one hand.

"Yes," he muttered. He glanced back at me, his face suddenly childlike without the heavy frames. Then he turned to watch the Kanonkop being rubbed into dusk by the setting sun. "A remarkable woman. She is very strong, and she believes in things. She has—" He thought for a moment. "She has very strong *principles.*"

A shotgun shattered the silence. Seconds later the parrots swept past the window. Five o'clock. Time for a beer.

Sandile's voice murmured on: Sylvia. Scheepersdorp. Now and then a word bobbed up and I held it for a while, turning it over a few times to inspect it more closely. Family. Leaders. The new South Africa. A good team.

Then Sandile stopped. He coughed again. "Connie," he said, "Constance. About your sister."

He took a deep breath, ready to spill it out at last. I tried hard to concentrate. Nothing like a dying woman to make people confess. They know you can only take their secrets to the grave.

But just then, the door opened and Bart came in with a tray of soup.

Chapter 14

ALMOST AS QUICKLY as the crowd around the bridge knitted together to watch Princess and Alwyn, it loosens and unravels again. People are heading in different directions: towards the taxi rank or the off-licence on Railway Road, or to the edge of Scheepersdorp where the N1 starts, ready to hold up cardboard signs with the licence numbers of towns they're headed for. Still shaking with kwaito, the taxi climbs the hill from Scheepersdorp towards the highway, a tower of cases balanced on its roof.

A slow sigh of relief ripples down Plumbago Way. Bolts slide back. Windows swing open again.

At number twenty, Esmé van der Walt finally stops counting the tins lined up on her garage wall. The beans will expire soon. Perhaps she can open one for Alwyn's lunch. Just to be safe, she takes two. Then she locks the garage and shuffles back to the house in her pink slippers. It feels safe enough, now, to open the lounge curtains. Esmé peers out of the window, just in time to see her son strolling up the road.

Thank the Lord, he is safe and well! From this distance, Esmé can't yet make out Alwyn's hair plastered to his crown, or the dampness of the towel draped round his neck. She must warm up the frying pan! For lunch she has planned stir-fry and brown rice to go with the beans: one of the healthy meals the doctors have advised her to make. But at that moment her phone starts to ring. Esmé hurries to answer it.

Ivor and Janice are nearing the hill towards home, Janice just a half-step ahead as she tries not to hurry him too obviously.

"I'm going over to Sylvia's later," Ivor says, as they approach the right turn into Bloubessie Way. "She asked me for a drink."

"Am I invited too?" Janice quickens her pace.

"Of course." Ivor puts his hands in his pockets and dawdles deliberately on the corner of Plumbago and Bloubessie. "Will you come?"

"Baby." Forced to stop, Janice still manages to look hurt rather than annoyed. "Of course I'll come. Why wouldn't I?"

"I know these things are difficult for you," Ivor says.

"What things?"

He jangles his keys in his pockets. "Sylvia. Marianne. They'll be talking about Connie. It's a year today."

"I know." Janice turns into Bloubessie and walks on without him, chipping her heels so sharply into the asphalt pavement that sparks almost fly. "I can't really forget the day Connie West died, can I?" she calls over her shoulder. "Our first wedding anniversary?"

"Shit." Ivor freezes. "How could I forget?"

"I don't know." Janice holds the front gate open for him to follow her. She doesn't quite manage to keep the chill out of her voice when she says, "Shall we go to bed anyway?"

Alwyn is ambling up the driveway of his mother's house. At the top of the stoep Esmé waits, flabby arms folded. She's just been on the phone to her friend Tinkie, who lives near the bridge, and she's ready to give her son hell. There's a hot bath and a clean towel ready for when she's done.

One, two, three! Up the polished green steps of the stoep Dr Mkhaliphi skips like a young man, his tie flying over his shoulder. Behind him, Alwyn follows, one step at a time.

In Esmé's bedroom, the lace curtains lift in the breeze, brushing across the pram parked next to the bed. The pram trembles from side to side as a mound rears up under the blanket like a caterpillar.

Bum first, she used to stretch up and stir from her sleep – a good long while before opening her mouth to let us know she was awake, we should come and fetch her, and where were we, all of us meant to be looking after her? It was like the tremors before an earthquake. So many times I watched Sylvia or Princess haul her out of the crib or the pram, planting her on their chests. When they put her on my lap I was shocked at how heavy she felt. Heavy and hot.

She'd no idea I was her mother, any more than Princess or Sylvia were.

Don't blame *me*. Look: I knew there were plenty of people in this town willing to look after her for me. I wasn't the only one capable of giving her a good upbringing. I knew Scheepersdorp would be up to the task. And you can see for yourself how well they're all managing. The child won't lack for anything.

Besides, how could I be expected to make a decision like that? I couldn't even choose between a Hunger-Buster Burger and fish and chips. How was I supposed to decide about the life of a child?

In any case, I was like Harry. I never could stand waste.

Chapter 15

Sylvia said, "You're looking peaky, Con. Are you sure you're eating properly?"

If I'd been in the mood, I'd have laughed. I mean, I'd spent most of my life looking out for my younger sister. Checking she was home on time, her homework done, that she ate a good breakfast, that the house was safely shut up at night. Mostly because I was terrified Harry would find a reason to make us move in with Letty and him. But I guess when Sylvia turned twenty-one, I felt I could relax and let her do what she wanted. Now I realised how her inherent bossiness had crept up on us without my noticing.

"Yes," I said, "thank you," and I yanked a clump of onion weed out without bothering to trace the roots.

"I am eating properly," I said. "I am sleeping properly. And my bowels are regular, too. Also," – I straightened up – "I am twenty-fuckin'-seven years old, and I think I qualify as a grown-up now."

"Constance," Sylvia sighed. She found a low boulder next to some khaki bush and sat down, crossing one substantial thigh over the other.

99

This, I realised, was one of her flying visits to check up on me, though she claimed she'd come to pick up clothes. She was hardly ever home these days, running around with Sandile, drumming up support for the country's first democratic elections. But living on my own never bothered me. I enjoyed it when Sylvia came home, but it wasn't long before I started itching to be alone again.

After a while, Sylvia had another go: "You okay, Con?" There were pinches of pink on her cheekbones.

I'd filled a whole bucket with onion weed and moved on to some Port Jackson striplings before she tried once more: "It's just, you just don't seem quite – *happy*, Con."

"Don't." I stood up to chuck another weed on the pile. "Don't let's have this conversation about what being happy means again, Sylvia. Let's not. I mean," I couldn't help adding, "are *you* happy?"

"I'm not sure," she considered. A dreamy look swam across her face. I knew exactly what she was thinking about. Or who. She caught me looking at her and snapped to attention.

"I'm not *un*happy," she said. "I'm not *angry* either. And you just seem to me so …"

"Angry," I said.

"Well, yes."

"I *am* angry." I threw the trowel down so hard it bit into the soil. "I'm angry at being treated like a child by my younger sister. I'm angry that this whole bladdy town knows my business even before I do. I'm *so* angry that I can't be left to sort out my own life without you sniffing around here trying to stop me embarrassing you. In fact, Sylvia," I was shouting now, but not enough to miss the twitch of Esmé van der Walt's kitchen curtain across the fence, "I'm not just angry. I'm *pissed off*."

"Tell me about it, Con," she pleaded as I marched off to the other end of the plot to fetch the compost and spade I'd brought down with me. "Alwyn says a problem shared is a problem split in two."

I knew she suspected something. I felt pretty sure Princess had been spreading skinder again. They weren't going to buy that story about me having gastro for the third week in a row.

I must have spent about half an hour digging under the yellowwood while I waited for Sylvia to leave. I only stood up and turned round when I heard the back gate to the plot squeak shut and Sylvia's car reversing down the long driveway.

She'd left a bag of groceries on the kitchen table for me. Healthy stuff: brown bread, cottage cheese, bananas. And a cucumber shrink-wrapped in green plastic. It was the only thing I felt like eating.

After I'd cut the cucumber up I arranged the slices on a blue plastic plate. I sat at the kitchen table in my grubby denims and turned each slice round to look at it before I put it in my mouth. Dark green ringing peppermint. I imagined them dissolving into my bones and my blood, colouring my veins, coating my heart with a smooth, lime-tinted skin. In my womb, a jungle of vines would grow over the minuscule bean-shaped parasite.

I knew how inconvenient this whole thing was going to be for everyone. I already had an inkling it would prove to be my undoing.

I also knew I wasn't going to do a single bloody thing to stop it.

Perhaps thirty years from now, my daughter will return to Plumbago Way. Maybe she'll pass through town with a lover or a friend, and they'll drive to the top of the street and park their car opposite number twenty-two. Marianne will point out her old bedroom, where a plum tree once grew. And the bedroom facing the Kanonkop, where her father (and before that her mother) slept. Once, she may tell her companion, that driveway ran straight to the top of the property, ending opposite the kitchen door. And there was a pergola with a purple bougainvillea tumbling over it, where her father parked an Isuzu bakkie each night. The one her mother left them when she died.

Perhaps Marianne will say that what she misses most of all is sitting on the wooden bench on the front stoep, and the trellis screening it. Her mother had planted a dipladenia to climb it shortly before she – Marianne – was born.

Marianne might say of her mother: my father says she hated Barbie dolls and pink. And flowers from English country gardens. But she told him the dipladenia would be okay if she grew it in a pot. She thought it was something a baby might enjoy. And Marianne may tell her friend how, to this day, the pink and yellow splash of dipladenia flowers gives her heart a pang.

Standing on my front stoep with Dr Mkhaliphi, I'm not bothered by his silence. It's easier to mock people who shoot their mouths off. Silence may be difficult to read, but I'm more comfortable with that than with meaningless words. Even though whenever I look Dr Mkhaliphi in the eye, I feel he's shutting me out. He's not going to give any information away. Not about me, not about him. Whenever I'm tempted to question him again, I can hear gates slamming and padlocks turning. And if I *do* dare ask, his eyes flatten to a dull, bark-coloured brown.

"G'n skaamte nie!" Esmé is shrieking at Alwyn next door. "No shame!"

From my stoep, Dr Mkhaliphi and I can hear every word. Now and then there's a low answering rumble from Alwyn, but it doesn't last long.

"What will people say?" Esmé screams. I don't have to look across to know how her pea-sized eyes are screwed up, her bust heaving under the pink housecoat. "Go climb in the bath!"

Dr Mkhaliphi doesn't let on he's heard any of it. He's standing on the top step in his pinstripe suit, back straight, shoulders square. The metal frames of his prescription glasses glint as I follow his gaze across the plot to Ivor's house.

"Oh, please," I sigh, "I forgive him. Alright? I forgive them both. God. What more do you want?"

I start counting the number of pink buds beginning to fatten on the dipladenia, wondering if Bart's been feeding it 2:3:2 regularly like I told him. "I don't know, I don't care, it doesn't matter," I whisper to myself. How long had I told myself that? But it's not true. Finally, I'm prepared to admit that. Perhaps it's the clue I've been waiting for.

Dr Mkhaliphi leans back against the wrought-iron railing of the stoep and folds his arms. It's not like time's a problem for *him*. And I know for sure he wants to hear everything.

As if he doesn't know already. As if he doesn't know the whole story that happened between Ivor and Bart and me.

It was the hottest summer in decades. The river had shrivelled to a lick on the river bed and the dams were shrinking daily under that screwing sun. We'd had one fire already, even though it was just the beginning of the season. At night we watched fires glowing on the Kanonkop, here, there, across the horizon, like they were taunting us.

I need you to come with me, Ivor yelled from the bottom gate that morning at five, just after he got the call. A couple of men caught in the fire at Bezuidenhout's farm had been injured.

He knew I'd be awake that early. I never could sleep late, especially not in summer.

Just as I was I climbed into his car, shorts and a tee-shirt, grabbing my boots and socks and pulling them on as he pulled off for Bezuidenhout's place.

In the end, there were just a couple of surface burns and a sprained ankle for Ivor to see to, and by seven-thirty they'd got the fire under control. While Ivor packed up his equipment and chatted to Bezuidenhout, I walked around the farm, working out what trees I could get to repair the damage.

What happened on the way home? We didn't talk much, I remember that. Believe me, I went over that short trip often enough in my mind afterwards, and never managed to turn up anything new. In the end I just erased it, like it was a video clip. I never played it again, or allowed myself to ask why things worked out the way they did that day, when everything had seemed the same as always.

I didn't have to work that afternoon, so when Ivor dropped me home, I decided to walk up the Kop to see from there how much damage had been done by the fire. When I told Alwyn I was going he was worried about cobras and puff adders fleeing from the heat, but I made sure to stomp hard to warn them as I went along. The earth on the path was so cracked and dry it didn't even raise dust under my feet.

There wasn't much shelter at the top. Most of the bushes were dried up or burned to the ground, and the best I could do was ease in under the shadow of the red-rocked Kop. It was eleven o'clock by then, so even that didn't cast much of a shadow for me.

Scheepersdorp, too, looked stripped naked and imprisoned by the heat. All the plants on the plot below seemed to droop. There was hardly anyone outside or on the streets. Though if you looked hard enough you could make out Bezuidenhout's men still hard at it on the other side, sacking the fields beside the farm.

Outside the corrugated-iron houses in Kangela Township on the opposite hill, children were playing. I caught the glint of their slippery bodies down by the river even though it was more mud than water by then.

Then my eyes travelled even further, to the chalky plume of dust spooling out between the hills where the dirt road branched off from the N1. The trail of dust was attached to a car: I caught glimpses of it as it wove in and out of the hills. A small red car. A Ford Cortina.

Just before the green-and-white national sign announcing the turn-off to Scheepersdorp, the car slowed down and stopped. Dust collapsed from the sky. A few seconds later, the driver's door opened.

Even from where I stood, it was impossible to miss those long legs unfolding from the car, the energy in those supple limbs. Maybe in time I'd look back and tell myself I'd already noticed, from that distance, the breathlessness, the eager way she pulled her camera out. That I may even have heard – on top of catching the white flash – the click of her camera as it sliced the Scheepersdorp sign into immortality. Maybe I did. Maybe I didn't.

What I know for sure is I never had any bad feeling or premonition about what I'd seen. I was just curious, that's all. We all noticed when a stranger came to town.

When I tell this all to Dr Mkhaliphi, it's like I'm apologising for something.

Chapter 16

EVERYONE THOUGHT THE first time I clapped eyes on Janice was the night of the disco at the Scheepersdorp Museum. They were wrong. I was bent over a tray of basil the first time I heard her voice. From that moment on, the smell of basil reminded me of Janice. I couldn't eat pizza without thinking of her.

When I stood up, I had to lift my chin to take her all in. Not just the height, but also because she was so – *peppy* – standing there in her designer jeans, her sunglasses perched on her head.

I was never a good judge of character. I never took to anyone on first meeting them. I was always too aware of their flaws: tea-stained teeth, say, or too much gum when they smiled. Or a habit of tweaking their nose before they spoke. I was always too distracted by things like that to see the person inside and I usually left disliking them.

What friends I had it took me a long time to get used to. To see past all their tics and flaws. Alwyn with his odd shuffle and chameleon eyes – well, I'd grown up with him, so that was okay. Bart with his ruddy cheeks and blistering white skin. Ivor's tense, compact way of carrying himself. Even my own sister repelled me sometimes, with her odours of sweat and salt and that wretched vanilla perfume.

Janice was different. She examined me, head inclined. When her ginger bob flopped forward, she tucked it quickly behind her ear. I had time to notice the freckles spanning her nose, and the shifting yellows and browns of her eyes. She didn't smile. Not at first.

Other people might have thought it rude, but I didn't mind. I liked it. It left space for me to relax a little. She wasn't even aware that she was staring. She was like a child who hadn't been taught to pretend.

"I want to grow some herbs in my flat," she said. "Will these be alright on my windowsill?"

She talked nervously, a sort of continual gabble. She kept asking me questions, then blushing. "It's good to meet you," – her eyes flicked over the name tag on my lapel, and for a moment she rested a hand on my muddy arm – "Connie. I hope we'll meet each other again soon."

"It's a small town," I smiled.

It had been Sylvia's idea to organise a dance at the Scheepersdorp Museum that night. Or so we thought. Only long afterwards did we discover it was really Sandile Sinto who wanted to raise funds for the new Khoisan exhibition. But at that stage, Sylvia hadn't even told us Sandile was back, let alone teaching in Kangela Township. Sylvia had been involved in township community meetings for some time, but we all kept quiet about it because of Harry and Toppie de Bruyn.

Sylvia organised for the main exhibition hall to be cleared out, and she got sponsors for snacks and drinks and a disco. With the wind of change in the air, a lot of people were keen to get on board and show they never voted for the National Party. At the golf club, Toppie started going on about how he'd just hired a woman as the new partner in his legal practice, and how Scheepersdorp would have to transform its old-fashioned ways. Toppie's wife Bets hoped having a woman business partner would teach Toppie to put the toilet seat down.

Sylvia put up posters for the museum dance in Main Road and the library and in most of the shop windows. By the second day, most tickets were sold. Alwyn was in charge of the bar, and Bart's Pub and Grill donated six crates of beer and four platters.

I got there late. After climbing the Kop, I'd gone back to Bezuidenhout's farm to deliver a load of saplings, and as usual I'd ended up staying to help plant them.

It was already eight o'clock when I finally pulled the Isuzu into my driveway. Then I still had to shower and change before walking down to the museum. I can't remember if I'd told Ivor I'd meet him there or not. I guess I just assumed I would.

Sylvia had said, *Green. Green suits you*, *Con*, dragging me out of the dressing room to the big mirror in La Femme Boutique. The dress displayed my cleavage perfectly, she said. And the length was just right. A hemline just above the knee showed my legs at their best, according to her. Even I could see how well the emerald fabric set off my sun-tanned skin and fair hair. Which Sylvia had managed to pile up in one of those buns (or 'chignons' as Janice called them) she was so fond of for herself. Of course, wisps of my hair were still sticking out at all angles. But I'll admit I liked what I saw.

Sylvia said the dress was her birthday present to me, though my birthday was months ago. She spent half her meagre salary on a green dress and white sandals with a small heel. *Really small*, Sylvia urged. I hardly ever wore heels.

That night was one of the few times I didn't take the short-cut across the plot to the centre of town. It wouldn't do for that expensive dress, those larney shoes to go tramping through the soil. Or swinging across the stream on an old rope. I kept my corduroy bag, though. Sylvia couldn't get me to part with that. It made me feel more myself, having it swung over the shoulder of my new green dress.

The mist down Main Road was fine as dandelion seeds, and houses and trees loomed up in sections at me: a shoulder of branch here, a glint of iron gate there. Even the *doef-doef-doef* of the disco was muffled by the soft mist. I remember looking down at my blurred toes peeping out of the new, white sandals tapping down the pavement.

The disco lights were already pulsing across the front lawn of the museum and I waited for a minute before going in. I looked at my shadow prickled into the grass of the lawn: angles of skirt and shoulder and piled-up hair. I wondered what Ivor would think.

I slipped in the back way. I wanted to check myself in the cloakroom mirror first. The chignon didn't feel a hundred per cent secure, and I was trying to stab it back into place with hairpins when I heard the cloakroom door swing open and the babble of party and music slice in. The toilet door bolted shut, and I heard silk rustle, followed by a heavy trickle.

The toilet flushed. The bolt slid back.

Even before her face moved into the mirror behind me I recognised her.

"It's you!" She clapped her slender hands. "I *knew* we'd meet again!" She wrenched the tap open. "How are you? Isn't this fun?"

"Great fun," I smiled. "I see you're getting to know the locals."

"Just like you told me, Connie." She'd remembered my name. But then, I'd remembered hers. "And the people!" Her voice echoed across the cloakroom. "Such nice people! There's Mr De Bruyn. Mr and Mrs Healey, and Alwyn, Alwyn—" Her teeth worried at her wide lip.

"Van der Walt," I said.

"Alwyn van der Walt and Bart Mayford; and Sylvia—"

"Sylvia West. My sister."

"You're *joking*." A hand landed on my arm. "Your *sister*! She's so *nice*. She's been introducing me to everyone."

"That's my sister." I started burrowing in my handbag, hoping someone would come in and interrupt us.

"And then there's that guy – shortish, sandy-coloured hair? Going white in front. The doctor." Janice primped her bob in the mirror, avoiding my eye.

"You mean Ivor Shepherd."

"Ivor Shepherd. Yes." She took her lipstick out and pursed her lips at her reflection. "He's *gorgeous*."

"Is he?" I stared at her for a few seconds. Then I zipped my bag shut and headed for the door.

"Is he involved with anyone?" Janice called after me.

I stopped at the cloakroom door because there didn't seem to be any reason to escape any more. Janice was leaning over the basin smearing lipstick on while she waited for me to reply.

"I'm not sure," I said at last.

"*Surely* you must know," Janice smiled at me from the mirror, "in a small town like this? I'm sure *everyone* knows everyone else's business, don't they, Connie? Your sister said so." She snapped the lipstick lid back on. "You don't mind if I call you Connie?"

"Ivor tends to be a private person," I said eventually. "He's not very public about who he's with."

"Is he?" She raised an eyebrow. "Is he, indeed? Seriously, though, I *would* like to know if he's involved with anyone. I don't want to cause trouble. Especially being new in town and all that. I wouldn't want to steal someone else's boyfriend."

"Boyfriend?" I'd always hated the word. What did it mean? Friend, boy, possession, fashion accessory?

I took in Janice and her red lipstick. I thought about the quietness and silence of the walk down the Kanonkop that afternoon. About how Ivor and I had worked together the entire morning without needing to say more than a couple of words to each other. There were other ways of showing what you meant to a person. He knew that.

"He's nobody's boyfriend," I told Janice.

I stood back from the door to let her clip-clop swiftly past me. Then I went back to the mirror to try and remember what Sylvia had taught me about fixing a chignon.

When I walked in through the double doors five minutes later, Sylvia and Bart were the first people I saw, and I pushed my way towards where they were dancing.

That Sylvia. Always worrying about everyone else. Bart had been in town three months already, but she *still* had to make sure he didn't feel left out of things. The two of them were out in the middle of the floor, Bart twirling Sylvia round so her dark hair flew up and flashed blue, green, golden in the disco lights.

At first I wondered why they seemed so excited to see me – I'd been with them only twelve hours before. Sylvia grabbed my arm and spun me round until I felt dizzy. I still wasn't used to heels, and every now and then Bart would have to clutch my elbow to stop me falling over.

Ivor never liked moving to music. He always looked like he didn't have enough time to decide where to put his arms and legs; like he'd got too used to the sharp movements of snipping and injecting and swabbing to be able to surrender to invisible sounds, to listen to what the music was telling him.

But Bart did. For a big man, he moved surprisingly well. He took my hands and pushed me out, then pulled me in again so I almost banged into his solid chest – but stopping me just in time. Then he took my hand in one of his and stepped me in a neat circle around him. It was easy to follow his lead: I didn't have to do anything except let him shift me where I needed to be. And when he moved like that, he was all neatness and control, not a hint of bulk or beer boep.

Both he and Sylvia must have known it was only a matter of time before I looked around. And when I eventually did glance across the room and see Ivor and Janice, I knew for sure every pair of eyes there was waiting to see what I'd do: from the people peering at me from the dance floor to the ones leaning over the bar waiting for Alwyn to pour another Klippies and Coke. I knew about all that stuff. I'd grown up in Scheepersdorp and I wasn't going to give anything away.

It was only a glimpse, but it was enough. You didn't need longer than that to work out what Ivor and Janice were up to. Her red nails digging into the back of his white shirt, her head lowered to burrow into his neck. He was just that crucial bit shorter than she was, even when she wasn't in black stilettos. It was a clear indication of what would follow later that night when they went home to Ivor's house, slamming his bedroom door on the rest of us.

I felt a pair of plump hands slide round my waist. Bart turned me to face him again. Step in, step out; my feet fell into line as he swung me in and out of the dance. He was grinning as he tucked me in next to him, then two-stepped me round again like I was a floppy doll. I suppose if anyone had looked closely enough, they'd have noticed how hard I was trying, but it was a dark room and the music was deafening.

When I eventually stopped and told him I was thirsty, Bart plunged through the crowd to the bar and came back with a beer. Then he grabbed my free hand and cleared a path for us to the verandah. Sylvia had disappeared by then.

Ivor and Janice had vanished as well. I'd been too careful

about making sure no one noticed me noticing them to be sure of exactly when.

It was cool and quiet on the verandah. When Bart flopped onto the steps beside me he was still breathless from dancing, and his shirt was wet with sweat. I could feel the heat coming off him.

"What did you say?" I asked.

"I said, 'He needs his head read.'"

"Who?"

"That guy." Bart tipped his big, dark head towards the front gate as if he'd just seen them leave. "Ivor."

"Ivor?" I realised I was shaking. "What do *you* know about Ivor?"

"Not much." Bart thought I didn't notice him shifting closer on the wooden step. "I heard you two were an item, though."

"Were." My voice was chilly.

"Until tonight, I'm guessing."

"Piss off." I took a swig of beer. "We've known each other a long time," I said after almost five minutes had passed. "We grew up together."

At that moment a conga line came chugging out of the dance hall. Sweaty and flushed, the dancers thudded across the wooden floorboards of the verandah, and Bart and I jiggled up and down as they passed. Second from last was Sylvia, hair flapping, mouth wide and dimpled with her famous smile. Clinging to her broad hip with one hand, Sandile Sinto grinned and waved at me with the other.

"She's a determined woman," Bart said when they'd disappeared inside again, "Janice."

"Janice?" I decided to play dumb.

"That's her name. Janice Eliot. Toppie de Bruyn's new partner. She set her sights on Ivor the minute he walked in."

113

"You were watching, were you?" For some time I'd suspected Bart noticed more than he let on. All that hanging round the bar polishing beer glasses and clearing plates from tables.

"Sure." Bart ignored my sarcasm. "She's hard to miss. And she's got great legs."

"Hard to miss in that mini. At least she had panties on."

"Red ones."

"Yes, thank you, Bart." But I'd glimpsed them too. From the corner of my eye, when "Twist and Shout" came on and Janice kicked out her legs. It was the only time you could've slid a knife between her and Ivor.

"Sorry." He nudged me so hard I had to lunge at my beer to stop it getting knocked over. "She's nothing on you though, Connie. Seriously."

I turned to stare at him. His plump bottom lip was pursed like he was about to laugh again, and his black curls were plastered onto his forehead with sweat. But instead of their normal, amused sleepiness, his blue eyes were narrowed and alert.

"You're making excuses for him? For Ivor?"

"Not excuses." Bart shook his head. "I wouldn't do that. Personally, I think he's an arsehole."

He slid his large backside down to the next step so he was sitting below me. "I don't know what's going on between you two," he said, gazing out at the hunched black shrubs of the museum garden. "I just think you should look beyond the obvious."

"Meaning?"

"Meaning this probably isn't about *you*."

I thought about that for a bit.

"I don't get you, Bart," I said at last. "You've only been in Scheepersdorp – what? – three months? And already you've sussed us all out."

"Gotcha!" He slapped my knee as he stood up. "I will never understand," – Bart stretched out his flabby arms, then folded them across his chest to look down at me – "why women always prefer bastards to nice guys. Like me."

Chapter 17

JANICE WANTED THE GARDEN RIGHT. An arch of roses for her and Ivor to stand under when they made their vows, a perfectly smooth green lawn. Lavender and jasmine. A willow tree. And roses, roses everywhere. Plus a brood of bantam hens to control pests and lay eggs for Ivor's breakfast.

On the morning of her wedding, she wanted to pick pink roses from her own garden for her bouquet. White iceberg roses for Ivor's corsage, and red ones – Mr Lincolns – to decorate the rich dark-chocolate cake she'd ordered for the reception.

She talked so fast I couldn't always make out what she was saying. She rushed at the words like she was weeding them out, or setting them up like a fence around all the things she wanted to control: Ivor, the garden. Me. And she made you believe she'd do it all, too. That almost anything was possible. "I believe Rome *can* be built in a day," I heard her tell the architect one afternoon.

Try as I might, I couldn't dislike her perfectly plucked eyebrows or her short, polished nails. Or her habit of tucking the fringes of her bob behind her ears when she got excited. There was something vaguely innocent about all these things.

I'm still not sure if at that stage Janice knew about Ivor and me. Though I did wonder if she only offered me the landscaping job to make me feel better about things. I suspect a lot of people saw it that way.

And I needed the work. Even though I spent most of my day delivering and selling plants and trees, I struggled to balance things at the end of each month, what with living expenses and the rates for the house and the plot. I knew I'd have to face the dilemma of selling the plot in the end, but I wanted to give it my best shot for as long as I could.

I gave up trying to persuade Janice to look at indigenous plants, and swotted up on roses and azaleas so I could give her exactly what she wanted. I put together a quote for an irrigation system that would water the property with the turn of a tap. I made lists, and a big diagram of a garden layout – we spent hours going over it. Janice wrote notes and corrections with a red pen, and I noticed her hand trembled as she drew.

At Ivor's back fence, bordering on the plot, my team dug a trench and filled it with manure from Bezuidenhout's farm. I drove the Isuzu to East London and fetched a willow sapling and the roses: pink and white icebergs and half a dozen Mr Lincolns, as well as a basket of ten bantam hens Janice had managed to track down. They scratched and pottered around us while we planted. One lay a clutch of eggs under the lavender bush, right next to the winding path of pebbles and sand Janice had designed.

She took to walking through the rose garden before breakfast each day with a cup of filter coffee and a clipboard and pen. Once or twice, she arranged to meet me there before I went off to the nursery. I was with her the morning she stopped suddenly and pointed down at the path.

"What's that?"

A slender, straight indentation in the middle of the carefully brushed sand about twenty centimetres long. It softened and blurred, then sketched itself again in the faintest print of scales below the lavender bush.

"It's the bantams," I said eventually, "their eggs. They're a temptation."

Sure enough, the bantam eggs had disappeared.

Janice freaked out big time. It was no use telling her to be aware, just make a noise when you walk down the path, lock the bantams in a hutch at night. She went on a complete mission. Got a yappy fox terrier that caused more trouble with the hens than anything else. And electric fencing. As if that would keep her visitor out. And she kept on at me about selling her the plot. I tried being polite – I was still uneasy with her – but in the end I made it clear I wouldn't sell. Not at any price.

"It can wait," Janice smiled. By then she'd calmed down a bit and her mind had started simmering with wedding ideas again. "One thing at a time."

Despite minor setbacks like this, settling in our town must have all seemed fairly straightforward to Janice at first. Too straightforward.

When she found out it wasn't that simple – that nothing in a small town ever is – I have to admit she showed guts. Even though Ivor gave her his body but never quite handed over the rest of him. Even though the garden rejected her roses and pansies and kept on spitting blackjacks and verbena and visitors from the plot back at her. Even though I betrayed and deserted her in the end.

That's how she chose to see it, anyway. In truth, I wasn't her friend to start with and I never pretended anything else. Good luck to her.

It's not easy to avoid someone in Scheepersdorp, but for a

long time I managed. Of course, there's the odd occasion when you can't help it, especially with everyone living so close to each other. And there were unavoidable meetings – when Janice asked me to advise her on her garden, for instance.

But I never spoke properly to Ivor again. I managed to arrange it so I saw him as little as possible, and mostly at a distance. I was at work all day, usually out of town, and if I felt like getting out in the evening I'd go down to Bart's place for a beer. Ivor and Janice tended to hang out more at the Royal or the country club, though once or twice I was trapped with them among all the others at Bart's. Sylvia always told me afterwards that I managed to put a good face on things.

In the end, someone must have tipped Janice off about Ivor and me, because I came home a few weeks before the wedding to find a note slipped under my front door. It was written in purple ink on lavender-scented paper. A thin, lopsided hand. Janice had had second thoughts about any more garden plans, but please would I bill her for the trouble I'd gone to so far. I never did.

I don't think Ivor would have told her himself, so I guess that caused some drama between the two of them. She would've wanted to know why he never spoke up about me. But it wasn't enough to spoil their wedding day. Not from what I understood. And the rose garden was well on its way by then.

After that, I mostly stayed home and read in my spare time. I'd finally got around to unpacking the last few boxes of books Maggie Shepherd left me. They'd been kept sealed up in the garage, and though I'd rummaged through them over the years, there were still four or five unopened. Two of them turned out to contain the Russians: Dostoyevsky, Solzhenitsyn, Tolstoy. I'd always wanted to read *Anna Karenina* and now seemed the right time.

The first time I opened the book, a strand of long, dark hair slipped out. On the flyleaf in spiky handwriting: *Margaret Marianne Scheepers. 14 Bloubessie Way, Scheepersdorp.* Maggie had been one of the original Scheepers.

I finished *Anna Karenina* in a week. Every night I'd come home from work, shower and change. Then, in my tracksuit and wet hair, I'd prop the book on the kitchen table to read while I ate the supper Sylvia usually dished up for me before she went out.

The last three boxes from Maggie were poetry. Mostly the Romantics, but also a couple of modern anthologies, and two Emily Dickinson collections. A lot of them had pages turned down, or were bookmarked with flattened foils from Stuyvesant boxes. Occasionally, Maggie had made a pencil mark in the margin of a verse she liked. There was one she'd underscored as well. It was a poem about despair. How, when we're trying to walk through it, the darkness either alters, or our eyes get used to it until we learn to step "almost straight" again.

When I read those lines, it felt like a door in my head had opened and someone had finally stepped inside. I imagined Emily Dickinson and Maggie Shepherd in my room with me: Emily with her diminutive feet dangling off the edge of my bed, Maggie with her back to us, smoking as she stared out the window.

Looking back, it seemed like I slowly dissolved into the pages of Maggie's books during the six months it took for the museum dance events to develop into Ivor and Janice's wedding day. I just disappeared into another world, where life was cruel and you either altered your step or threw yourself under the Saturday express from PE to East London. Needless to say, I did neither.

Scheepersdorp was captivated by the frenzy and romance of the wedding. This made it easier for me to fly under the radar, stay home and read. I was never the biggest presence in a room, anyway. I figured once I got through the wedding and things settled down again, I could start facing the idea of seeing Ivor and Janice as a couple.

Ivor and I saw each other at a distance now and then – how could we not? – but usually one of us was able to duck into a shop or a side street, or dawdle until there was enough distance between us. It was a good five months after the wedding when I finally bumped into him in the parking lot outside the Nest Café one afternoon. Literally. I opened the door of the bakkie as he walked past. I genuinely hadn't seen him coming.

"Fucking hell," he hissed, clutching his stomach. Then, "It's not bloody funny."

"I didn't say it was." But I still couldn't stop laughing. I grinned up at him from the driver's seat. "Sorry. It was just the way you said it."

"How was that, then? How did I say it?" I couldn't see his eyes behind his sunglasses, but the two lines beside his mouth were pulled down in a scowl.

"You said *ing*. Fuck-*ing*. Everyone else round here says *fukken.*"

Ivor placed a hand on the top of the open bakkie door.

"How are you?" he asked.

"Fine." I stopped laughing. "Very well."

I thought Janice might be with him, that maybe he'd want to hurry and catch up with her so she wouldn't see him talking to me. But he stayed hovering, his shadow breaking over where I sat in the hot cab of the bakkie.

"How's Bart?" he asked.

"Bart who?"

"Very funny," that tight smile of his, "everyone knows about you two."

"This *is* Scheepersdorp," I said.

"Good for you, Con. Seriously." Ivor took his sunglasses off so

I could see how earnestly he meant it. His hard blue eyes squinted down at me.

"He deserves you."

"Oh? And what does *that* mean?"

"Only good things."

"Well, then I shall say thank you." I swung a foot out, but he still didn't budge.

I placed a hand on top of the bakkie door, a safe distance from his.

"Can I go now?" I asked.

"Sure." And he stepped aside.

I had no choice, then. I had to stand up.

Even if he hadn't been a doctor, he'd have known.

Bart said, "You still love him, Con."

"You'd know, wouldn't you?"

It used to work on my nerves, the way Bart always *knew* everything. Ever since he arrived in Scheepersdorp, he'd been trying to pack me and Ivor and Sylvia and Alwyn into boxes so he could label us: rebellious; repressed; hippy; country bumpkin.

"Tell me then," he asked cheerfully, "what *do* you feel about Ivor, Con?"

It was the least I owed him, I knew that. But how could I explain things then? It seemed a little late for all that.

Once, I tried walking him up the Kanonkop, by way of starting the conversation. I thought it might be easier to talk when we weren't looking at each other. But Bart said it wouldn't be good for me, I'd never make it that far. Something might happen to the baby. He told me Alwyn had seen a leopard there the week before.

I said, "Don't you know Alwyn by now? It was probably Letty Healey's Labrador Fritz."

In the end I managed better than he did, even though at that stage I was almost as heavy as him. Bart's thick, strong legs might look like they were made for weightlifting, but he never cared to strain them.

He kept saying how tired and pale I looked, and I kept telling him I was pregnant, dammit. I couldn't stand him fussing over me.

Of course I was also sick by then, though he didn't realise that yet. I knew as soon as he found out he'd start pestering me. *Why? When? What are you going to do? Why didn't you tell me before?* He was bound to be hurt I hadn't told him earlier, and he had a right to feel that way. But I just didn't want to think about it any more, and I certainly didn't want to think about it with anyone else. Not even Bart. Especially not Bart.

I tried not to show how relieved I was when we got to the top. I'd taken a walking stick, but it was still heavy going. The path seemed steeper than before. We walked back without speaking, and when we got to the house, Bart stamped up the back steps and onto the stoep so the floorboards shuddered.

But it was never too difficult to jolly him out of things. One cold Castle and things would be back to normal again. He wasn't like me. He didn't believe in digging up old bones.

"What exactly are your feelings about Bart?" asked Sylvia. She kept pushing her wine glass a couple of centimetres to and fro across the kitchen table with her fingertips.

"He's a nice guy, Con," Sylvia sighed. "Don't write him off because the rest of us like him." She reached for the leather satchel she'd dumped on the table. She was off with Sandile again. Fundraising, my eye.

Before she left, she stood in the kitchen doorway for a moment. The last rays of sun were streaming through the door behind her and they highlighted the mass of dark, curly hair she'd recently stopped blow-drying straight. Her eyes and mouth were blotted into purple shadows, but for a moment I could almost see what people meant when they said my sister was beautiful.

But it didn't matter, because she was still Sylvia inside. And that's why she turned and left me alone in the dark.

Chapter 18

It's one-thirty on a Saturday afternoon in Scheepersdorp. By now, most people have eaten their hot dogs or homemade soup or Bart's Hunger-Buster Burger and they're settling down for the afternoon. *Pok, pok* go the tennis balls at the courts across the road. Two kilometres away, at the Scheepersdorp Country Club, Toppie de Bruyn swishes his driver, about to tee off. He's wondering if Harry Healey will make it to the course today.

At the Royal Hotel on Main Road, the bar's jam-packed and the TV's been switched on for the big match. The Scheepersdorp Museum is locking up its thick stinkwood doors for the day. And Marianne West has woken from her nap.

For a few seconds a wail rises above Plumbago Way, hovering above the tolling of the St Andrew's church bell. Then both sounds dissolve into the thin blue air.

Dr Mkhaliphi hasn't said anything while I talk to him. He's not like Sylvia or Esmé, always interrupting with questions or exclaiming *My hemel!* or *Of course not!* or *You're joking!* when I'm trying to finish the story. Dr Mkhaliphi just closes his long, sloped eyes while I talk. He doesn't even say *And then what?* when I stop to think. He knows I'm set to carry on till the bitter end.

Marianne. She must have been born with a frown on her face. That day, Sylvia stood beside my bed and lowered her arms for me to see what she was holding. The tiny face opened its eyes at me. It pulled down the corners of its wide mouth and sneezed. Then clenched fists and closed eyes again. As if she didn't like looking at me.

Babies on TV all woke from their afternoon naps with a gummy smile and a dry bottom. Not Marianne. For the first few months nobody got any rest. She'd curl up her miniature legs and her arms the size of chicken wings like they were pumping her mouth open, ready to let rip. And let rip she did, belting out a bawl you could hear even above the parrots coming in. Poor Sylvia. She walked that long passage for hours. At midnight, Bart took over. If Marianne was still yelling by the time he came home from the pub, he'd put her in the pram and walk her around town till she settled. I could hear the howl moving on down the driveway and into Plumbago Way, dwindling as Bart took a left and walked along Bloubessie to Main.

It was a bit easier in the day, when Princess strapped Marianne to her back with a blanket. Even then, one moment Marianne's head would be lolling, eyes shut, on Princess's back; the next her eyelids would screw tighter and her mouth would widen to release that spine-chilling din.

Today's no different. Even though Esmé has lifted the baby to her generous chest, desperate to console, to be the one Marianne holds arms out for; even though Alwyn is all but doing a tap-dance across his mother's bedroom floor to distract; there's only one person Marianne wants. Sure enough, within seconds, Princess appears magically in Esmé's bedroom door. Back in housecoat and doek, she looks like she hasn't been out today, though she's still wearing my black court shoes. In a trice she's got Marianne strapped to her back with a thick towel, jiggling her as she sings. If she's aware of the poisonous looks Esmé directs her way, she doesn't show it.

There's something I want the Boatman to know. Or perhaps I need him to explain it to me. That song Princess is singing. The one she was humming at the river: *Ndiza kukuncedisa uku-goduka*. Finally I remember when I've heard it before. Those last months, when I kept nagging Princess to help me. That's when she'd sing those lines to me.

Now the tune reminds me how it felt to have blood push against skin. And how I had no say in it: the in-breath, the out-breath. No matter what *I* wanted, my body just carried on in its own sweet way. Veins swelled up and subsided again. Sweat pushed out salt. Urine gushed out, warm. That heart that insisted on beating, night and day. Yet all over my body, microscopic timers had been planted, all of them ticking towards deadlines.

I try getting closer, to make out more of the words. But each time I approach, Princess manages to push me away.

I felt so cold the winter before Marianne was born. Every night I'd soak in a hot bath. Sometimes Bart would sit on the closed toilet seat to talk to me. He'd moved in with Sylvia and me by then.

"They say it's bad for babies to have water that hot," said Bart, himself puce from the run he'd committed himself to, sweat still seeping out. He was going to be a father now. Had to take care of himself, didn't he?

"So sue me." I strained myself up to twist the tap and let more hot water in.

Bart was so easy to read. *Shall I scrub your back, then, Con?* he'd ask. *Squeeze you some orange juice, maybe? Let me help you out of the bath.* Then – he could take a hint, our Bart – gradually shutting down. He just made the goddamned orange juice, put it on the edge of the tub without saying anything. Fetched milk and bread without being asked. Paid the bills. Ignored the outbursts and sarcasm.

Sylvia always said I could be hot as Hades if I wanted to. And cold as ice.

I'm not trying to make excuses. I treated him badly. But I had reasons for behaving the way I did, even though none of them were Bart's fault.

One day, just before I finally told him and Sylvia about my visit to the doctor in PE, Bart was trying to assemble the do-it-yourself cot he'd ordered. He'd been straining all morning to get it right, and still managed to leave out a couple of crucial bolts. One of them rolled under the grate of the old-fashioned fireplace, and when Bart stood up to get it he banged his head against the mantelpiece.

"Very funny," he said. I'd been watching from the doorway. Then, "I'm glad the first laugh you've had in months is at my expense."

"Sorry." But I couldn't stop.

"No, you're not." Bart rubbed his thinning crown. "You're not sorry at all."

That stopped me. "What do you mean?" I asked.

"You're not sorry to see me hurt. You like it." He picked up the hammer and turned it over in his chunky hands. He might have been speaking to that hammer, not me, lingering uneasily in the doorway.

"What are you talking about, Bart?"

"You're not happy about me. And you're certainly not happy about having this baby with me. I know that." He slapped the hammer against his palm as he spoke.

"I've never made any secret of that," I said quietly.

"No," Bart smiled. "No, you've never made any secret of

that," – his voice was light again – "but you *did* decide to have it, in the end, Connie. Constance." He shook his head. "What a name. What a name they chose for you. Constant."

"Constantly crabby."

"That, too."

"Thanks."

"Pleasure." It was so crisply said, so clearly pushed out, there was nothing I could think of saying back.

It was Bart who finally broke the silence. "I wonder why?" he murmured. He'd found the bolt by then, and was crouched on the floor, twisting it onto the screw.

"Why what?"

"Why you've decided to have this baby. There was always the other option."

"You mean abortion?" I put my hands in the small of my back and slid my feet coolly towards the opposite side of the door frame. "I've wondered about that, myself. I certainly thought about it. I suppose in the end I'm just too much of a coward."

I'd seen how he was with kids. They always made a beeline for him. They loved the way he turned into a kid himself: chasing them around, roughhousing. Teaching them how to shoot a catty or climb a tree. His own sweet tooth and the packets of jelly babies he kept in the cubbyhole of the Peugeot to share with them.

It would have been easy to remind Bart of that. But I didn't have the nerve.

He was so observant normally. So quick to pick up this and notice that. Sometimes he even had a strange way of knowing things *before* they happened. I didn't have to nod or shake my head; Bart could tell by my expression when something was wrong, when some strand between us had got twisted. But just not that time. Not the one time I most wanted him to see.

Chapter 19

"OF *COURSE* I WANT CHILDREN," Ivor says.

Standing on my front stoep, Dr Mkhaliphi's pupils contract. It's the only sign he's heard Ivor, because he doesn't turn or take his eyes off me, sitting opposite.

Things aren't going as planned at number fourteen. Janice has closed the bedroom door that opens onto the passage. Her sandals and top are off, and she's perched on the edge of the bed in skirt and bra. She's folded the blouse up into a square and she's pressing it down on the bed with her hands like it's a patient needing resuscitation.

Ivor's got his back to her. He's leaning against the frame of the French doors Janice had installed, staring out at the rose garden and the new water feature in the centre of the path. He hasn't taken his jacket off. Even after two years, it's clear he's itching to light up a cigarette.

He says, "I wish there wasn't so much pressure, that's all."

"We've been trying for two years, Ivor. We're not getting any younger."

"You're not *that* old, Janice. And there's nothing wrong with us. We just need to relax a little."

Reflections of light from the water feature jiggle and swirl across the ceiling, clear as what Janice is thinking now: *Yes. This is my fault. For being too uptight. For wanting this so badly. For wanting nothing else. I'm being punished.*

"I'm just not in the mood," Ivor says.

And since when, Janice wonders, was it so important to be in the mood? She stops herself from counting the number of times she had a headache, when she was tired, when … she twists the last button into its hook at the top of the blouse.

"I'll take you out to dinner tonight," Ivor says. He hasn't even heard her open the door to the passage again. From the top of the Kop, a caterwaul of parrots muffles the clink of a sherry decanter in the lounge. "Maybe after that we can try."

"You *know* it will be too late by then." Janice lounges in the doorway, pink-faced. She slumps onto the bed once more, hair flopping over her eyes. Her hand stretches out for Ivor to sit next to her "Honey, what *is* it? I know something's worrying you." Her fingers stray down, unbuttoning his shirt.

"Is it Connie?" she asks. "Are you thinking about her?"

"What? No," Ivor snaps. "What makes you think that?"

"It wasn't your fault, you know. That Connie died."

"What are you talking about, Janice?" Ivor clamps a cold hand over hers. "I never even treated Connie. She was my friend."

"More than that, from what I hear." Janice's voice is dry.

"What does *that* mean?"

Janice straightens up and tucks her hair behind her ears. A blush travels from her creamy cheeks down her neck. "Come on, Ivor. You're not going to tell me there was nothing going on between the two of you? How stupid do you think I am? This is Scheepersdorp, you know. No, what I'd like to know …" When Ivor still doesn't speak, she pushes on: "What I'd like to know is just when you planned on telling me yourself. About you and Connie. Or did you think I wasn't important enough?"

"Not you. Her. It," Ivor says eventually. "*It* wasn't important enough." He sighs. "It was all over between Connie and me long before you came here. Jesus, Janice," – she's dropped her head again and he tips her chin up between finger and thumb to look her in the eye – "have you been drinking?"

"And if I have, would you blame me?" Janice's eyes well up. "If I *were* to turn to drink, could you honestly say I had no reason? I mean: here I find I've been married two years and my husband never told me about the woman he was involved with for over a decade!"

"The dead woman," Ivor says.

"As if that sorts it out! Did you think I wouldn't need to *know* that? Did you think that wouldn't be important information for someone living in this town?" Janice takes a deep breath. She tries to exhale like she's been taught in yoga.

"Just tell me, Ivor," she says. "Just tell me once and for all what went on between Connie and you." She picks up his hand and threads her fingers through his. "I'm begging you, baby. We *can't* move on till we've sorted this out."

Answer the question please, Ivor. We are waiting. The purple light from the clouds outside has splintered across your face, and it's pooling in the creases at your eyes and the corner of your mouth.

There's no one here but you and Janice, Ivor.

And me.

And the Boatman, of course.

The truth, now.

What *was* going on between you and me?

* * *

I can't say he never laughed or enjoyed a joke, but generally he had a look that was stern and kind of solemn, and it seemed to suit him. When he *did* crack a smile, it began in a sly, shy kind of way. It felt almost shocking to see it splinter across his face, then move on through the rest of his body.

He never put his arm around me in public, like he did with Janice, or opened the car door, or steered me to a table with his hand in the small of my back. That's probably why for a long time nobody suspected there was anything between us. If we're talking about odd matches – like Bart and me – that would have been one for Scheepersdorp to wonder at too.

But for my part, it started the night I took Ivor across the plot. After that, it was all over for me. I gave him all my secrets, dropping them at his feet like a dog: the tilapia in the river and the best way to fish for them; the ant nests and the giant earthworms. How to read the tracks of guinea fowl and otter. The rare, soft-edged dent where a puff adder had slept on the dusty path after a hot day. The trek up the Kanonkop. The places where the bulbs came up each spring. And of course how to hide cigarettes and home-brewed pineapple beer under the yellowwood tree.

It made no difference that Ivor went off to university and I stayed behind in Scheepersdorp. The moment he came home for holidays he was off across the plot, yelling my name. Within minutes we'd be climbing the Kanonkop or running across the plot to check out all the stuff I'd been waiting to show him. At home, paging through the diagrams in his medical textbooks, he explained how the heart chambers worked, and the bones of the feet.

And of course there were the practical sessions, too. That started long ago, towards the end of my matric year, when he was eighteen and I was six months younger. Birds do it, bees do it, and

Ivor already knew then about making sure we didn't make any mistakes. And we never did.

I never worried about it. He said I should trust him and I did. I thought at least I had that kind of thing sorted. I thought I knew how to work the odds.

Until the morning Princess came in and caught me throwing up my guts in the bathroom at the end of the passageway.

A couple of weeks later, when I came home one night, Bart was waiting in the TV room off the kitchen. Sylvia had let him in before she left. He'd switched all the lights on and the house was blazing like it was midday, the TV on full blast while he watched a rugby replay. He tried to act casual when I walked in and dropped my keys and bag on the kitchen table, but I knew he was itching to find out.

On the floor next to him was a brown paper bag from Scheepersdorp Pharmacy.

I don't know what made me tell Bart I was over a month late. I hadn't even told Sylvia. But like I said: Bart had a way of picking up emotions. Even though we'd agreed we were seeing each other strictly as friends, he knew something was wrong and he kept going on and on till he managed to worm it out of me. From the moment I told him, he was on my case until I agreed to do a home pregnancy test. Of course, I had to get him to go and buy the stuff. If *I'd* gone into the only pharmacy in town to buy a pregnancy test, the phone lines across Scheepersdorp would have been humming within seconds of me leaving the shop. Bart wouldn't have been much better, so in the end he got his tea lady Agnes to do it for us. He sent her off to Scheepersdorp Pharmacy with a long list of stuff, and slipped the pregnancy test in the middle. He hoped they'd think it was for one of his staff. Of course, that would still set tongues wagging, but at least it put them off the trail for a bit.

That night, Bart handed me the packet without a word, and I went and shut myself in the bathroom. When I opened the bag I saw he'd bought two kits, to make absolutely sure. So I tested twice, and after ten minutes I went back to where Bart was sitting. He switched the TV off and I held the sticks up for him to see the two pink lines running down the middle of each.

"I'll move in here," he said eventually. From the TV room, his eyes followed me around the kitchen. Bottle, glass, corkscrew. I looked up from the cutlery drawer and he added, "If you like."

Of course I said no. And when he offered a few months later, I said no again. Then I let him change my mind. There were other factors to consider by then.

You could say it wasn't fair what I did to Bart. That I took advantage. And you'd be right.

But maybe he *wanted* to be taken advantage of.

He moved in four months before Marianne was born. Sylvia and Princess and I cleared out the spare room for him, next to mine. He fitted in better than I expected. He didn't push me too much and he tried hard not to cramp my style. When I got too heavy to climb the Kop, he'd walk down to the plot with me when he got back from work in the afternoons, before his evening shift. I'd show him what was new, what was budding, and where to find the bulbs I'd planted from the Kanonkop. I wondered at first if he was taking the piss, listening so carefully, but he seemed genuine. He was pretty helpful around the house, too. Some nights I'd sit out on the stoep and listen to him singing while he washed the supper dishes. He had a reasonably good voice and he knew all the really old songs: "Suikerbossie" and "Bobbejaan Klim die Berg". I found it weird he should sing them, but also sort of comforting.

Before I went in to help him dry up and put away, I couldn't help looking across the plot to the house opposite. Even though the iceberg roses had died off one by one, the willow tree Janice had planted had grown so lush in the summer rains it was difficult to make out the silhouettes flitting back and forth across their kitchen window. I'd wait for Ivor's figure to appear at the kitchen sink when he, too, did the washing up. Sometimes – I didn't imagine it – he'd stop for a minute and look out to where I was sitting on my stoep.

Chapter 20

"DID YOU HEAR THAT?" asks Bart. He's standing in the kitchen with a towel wrapped around his waist.

From her ironing, Princess glances through the kitchen window. A deep rumble rolls from the sky's throat, a sound like giant boulders scraping against each other. Seconds later, lightning convulses over the Kanonkop. A shattering crack. Jakkals shoots down the passageway and Marianne pinches Bart's bare leg to be lifted.

"Is the rain coming." Princess rests the iron on its stand. Before Bart can adjust his towel, she bends to pick up Marianne.

I caught her praying over me once. Princess.

She thought I was asleep but I woke up and saw her standing there with her head back, moaning, her eyes rolled up so you could only see the whites. The Hoover had been dropped next to the overturned rubbish bin.

Under no circumstances, I told her. *You keep away from me with that stuff. Not you, not anyone else. I catch you doing that again you're fired.*

Well, she was careful not to do it in front of me again, but I can't vouch for what happened when she was alone. She had a way of knowing better. Like the morning I caught her down by the plot with a garden trowel in one hand and Marianne's dried-up stump of an umbilicus in the other.

She wanted Marianne to know where she came from, she said. She pointed at my belly. *Inkaba yakho iphi? It means, where is your – this.* She drew nearer and placed a cold finger over the exact spot where my navel lay under my thin shirt. *When the people they ask Marianne, where did you bury this?* – she prodded my navel again – *then they know where she belongs.* Without another word she squatted down to dig. Right there in front of me, she buried the umbilicus under the yellowwood tree.

Did she know what had happened under that tree? Nothing would surprise me less. She was always mixing potions or saving dried-out chicken bones for her muti. On Saturday mornings people queued outside her room to consult her. Bart and I even caught Alwyn shuffling around there a couple of times.

It didn't matter. I was too tired to argue with Princess by then. And in a way, I was starting to understand what she meant, about belonging to a place. I still don't know where we go when we're dead, but I wouldn't have minded finding a way to stay part of the land where I began.

Besides, we all knew nobody could fire Princess. Not even Harry. Whenever he came over and told her to pack her bags, Princess just carried right on vacuuming. Or she'd yell over the Hoover at him: *I not going till Miss Letty she say I must go.*

When I bent, once again, over the toilet to hurl my guts up after Marianne was born, Princess just scooped the baby up and disappeared into the kitchen with her. Later, lying on my bed, I heard her go back into the bathroom to clean up. She had Marianne on her back and she was singing in Xhosa. Something about sleeping and your mother and I'll help you to rest. She told me it was a song she'd made up for Marianne even before she was born.

She's singing it now. The Boatman and I can hear it eddying up the passageway as Princess rocks Marianne on her back.

Harry Healey's study walls are lined with photos of mayoral dinners. Right in the middle is a framed hole-in-one certificate from the Scheepersdorp Country Club. Scattered across his desk are an open file and numerous hand-written scraps of paper, ready for Letty to type up. Then they'll be corrected by Harry and typed up again. Harry does not believe in computers and their sly convenience.

If re-elected Mayor, I will bring a wealth of knowledge and technical expertise to the running of Scheepersdorp. As a man of vast experience, and a native of Scheepersdorp of many generations – but already Letty's arthritic hands are scraping all the pieces into one thick bundle. She must hurry. If she can smuggle them out without Harry seeing, she can burn them with the compost later.

"Did you close the bathroom window?" she calls as Harry limps down the passage towards the kitchen. You can barely hear his footsteps over the slap of rain on the roof. Harry's not sorry he decided to give golf a miss today.

"It will be good for the garden," Letty says.

She's on the back stoep now, watching the rain ricochet off the leaves of the pecan-nut trees. She waves at Bart and Marianne on the back stoep of number twenty-two. She won't tell Harry she's just seen Sylvia and Sandile climbing the steps of my old house, curiously unhurried though the rain is bucketing down.

At Sandile's house across the river, the rain blurs the peeling outlines of the walls, and tries, without much success, to hush the tremble and shudder of the beat inside.

*   *   *

"Ma won't in any case see what I mean."

Alwyn is towel-drying his hair after his bath. Every few minutes, Esmé, who is short enough to fit under his arm, shunts him aside to attack the kitchen sink again. She keeps finding a spot she's missed.

"Ma?" Alwyn insists. "I mos just wanted to say thanks. Ma's always saying a person should be grateful for a person's health."

"Never. Skaamteloos. Never in my life so ashamed." Esmé is scrubbing so hard, her dumpy body jiggles from head to toe. "What will the people say?"

Chapter 21

ALWYN COULDN'T WALK BY THEN, so I'd go over to his place whenever I could manage. I was so cold that day, I pulled on two pairs of socks under my sheepskin slippers, then my sheepskin jacket and a beanie for my bare head. Four o'clock and it was almost dark. I picked my way down the front driveway, trying not to get my slippers wet. All over Scheepersdorp smoke was floating from chimney pots.

Esmé was surprised to see me. Also embarrassed. Most people felt that way when they had to look at my bald scalp and my clothes hanging off me. I often suspected I was a bit of a nuisance, making them so uncomfortable. Alwyn knew about that stuff.

The lights in his bedroom hadn't been switched on yet, and he was lying in the dusk. He hadn't got up for days. For a while I stood in the doorway watching him. His long legs were stretched out under the crocheted counterpane, his feet forming a large peak at the bottom of the bed. It was hard to watch the blankets over his chest: they took forever to swell up, and even longer to stagger down again. I tried to ignore the rasping sound that went with it.

I sat beside the bed counting the rows of pale faces in the old photos on the wall opposite. Alwyn's dad had played rugby for Border long ago, and there was a time everyone hoped Alwyn would step into his boots.

In the kitchen, Esmé clattered tea things and talked to her cat in the same wheedling tone she used for Marianne. All I could concentrate on was Alwyn's breathing. It sounded like gravel swishing under a wave. Then I started listening to the ocean of my own heartbeat. It seemed like the room was full of nothing but dead things – pictures, blankets, wood, wool – except for our battling breaths.

"Connie." I didn't know he was awake until he spoke. "Howzit. Is Ma making tea?"

"Ja." I took his hand. It was cold and clammy. "No news yet?"

"No news." Another slow, rasping breath. "Shit, Connie. Bladdy kak to find yourself hoping someone will have an accident, hey?"

"Don't think that way, man. Some things we just don't understand. I only wish," I fumed, "I could give you mine. God knows it's not going to be much use to me."

"That would be nice, hey Con. But I scheme," his eyes bulged at me, "I scheme you should keep it a while." He was shivering again and I started rubbing his hands.

"Shift up, you bugger." I kicked my slippers off and slid between the heavy layer of blankets and sheets, tucking them around the two of us.

When Esmé came in she nearly dropped the tray. "Liewe Here, Connie! Wat maak jy daar in die bed met die kind! Klim uit! Get out!" But in the end she propped a cushion behind Alwyn and poured tea in a saucer and blew on it, feeding him with a teaspoon while she held a dishcloth under his chin. She told us Harry had sent some pecans over for Alwyn. From the whole tree he'd only managed to collect one bag in a week. Esmé was going to make a pie, but two hours later Harry came and took the nuts back. The SPCA had been to see him: they had some wounded parrots to feed, and someone told them Harry kept a good supply.

After he drank his tea, Alwyn fell asleep again. Esmé went back to the kitchen and I stayed on, sipping tea and staring at the photos on the wall. I watched the light hunker closer to the shadows till it was almost completely dark. From next door, I could hear Princess calling me, and Bart's car pulling in. The creak of the gate as he opened it and drove through, then shut it again. Bart's footsteps down the driveway, also looking for me. *Crunch, crunch, crunch.*

"Connie," Alwyn said, "do you believe in heaven?" His eyes were still closed.

I could have lied. Told him all the things Esmé kept going on about. Green fields and sunshine. A bearded man in a long white cloak. Open-armed angels. But I was tired of pretending by then.

"No," I said at last.

"What do you think happens to us, Con?" When Alwyn opened his eyes for an instant, they were that blazing, cat's-eye green again.

"Well," – I realised I was still holding the cold teacup and I clinked it back onto its saucer – "I'll tell you what I *don't* believe, Alwyn. I don't believe there's a pretty forest in the sky with castles and a white light and God and all his angels waiting to welcome all the good people in. And you and me standing there sick with nerves while they check us out to see if we've made the grade. That sounds too much like immigrating to Australia. To be honest," and I glanced at him, afraid of how bleak I sounded, "I haven't the faintest bloody idea where we go when we die."

I couldn't tell if he was listening still, or if he'd fallen asleep.

But I couldn't stop myself from going on. "Other than that we disintegrate and our blood and bones slowly rot and feed the earth. And I like that idea," I said viciously. "I like the idea of my flesh feeding the soil and a thorn tree growing extra tall because of that. Or an aloe. Or a yellowwood. Apart from that," – I was starting to feel bad – "I'm not sure. I suppose I'd like to believe that all the things that made other people love you linger on. Like me." Even though I suspected he was asleep again, I grinned at him. "All the things you love about me, Alwyn. Like the way I treat Bart. And my sarcasm. And the horrible jokes I make."

"Con," he said quietly, "I'm serious, man."

I felt really bad, then.

"There are good things about people," I said at last, "and I believe they carry on, maybe like a plant. They seed themselves and grow again."

"Connie." He was staring at me again, lifting his head as he struggled to breathe. "Con … if there is. If we. What I mean is …"

"If I go first?"

"Ja. No. I mean … it's probably going to be me, ou Con. And if it is … listen to me now, Con."

I waited for him to finish. I hadn't planned on interrupting.

"I'll send you a signal." Alwyn fell back, exhausted.

Of course I wanted to ask: *Where? Get where first? Are we booked on the same flight? Can I fly business class?* But I didn't.

"Sure," I sighed. "Sure, Alwyn man. Why don't you do that." He waited.

"And if I go first," I said eventually, "I'll send you a message too. What will it be?" I lowered my head to whisper in his ear. "What would you like me to send you, hey? A big steenbras? A falcon?"

"Hey, Con." Alwyn closed his eyes. A grin swam over his face, then sank again. "You send me anything, bokkie. Whatever it is, I'll know it's from you."

Chapter 22

THE WINDOWS OF MY old house have flattened in the rain and every now and then a blurred figure moves across one of them. Footsteps hurry down the passageway. I recognise Sylvia's heavy tread and Sandile's long, light stride. A door opens and slams shut. Between flashes of lightning, a baby's cry flares up.

"No, no, no," shrieks Marianne from her high chair in the kitchen. Princess is pushing Smarties into her hand while Bart tries to snip her fringe with a pair of rounded scissors. I linger at the kitchen window, watching.

"Am I warmer yet?" I ask. Behind me, Dr Mkhaliphi runs a finger over a leaking seam in the kitchen gutter.

"You *are* warmer." He looks up. "I am happy to say you are warmer at last."

"Braver than you thought."

"Oh, no," he says, examining his muddy fingertip. For a moment I think he might even smile. Though I don't feel like smiling, myself.

"What about you?" I ask, though I'm still nervous of offending him. "Have you worked out why *you're* here with me?"

He doesn't reply. He's waiting for me to carry on. And he's

watching the rain spin down, shattering onto the driveway's fallen bougainvillea flowers and the glistening blue tar of the road.

Don't think I went down there deliberately. I would never have thought to see Ivor there. He didn't go many places without Janice any more, especially not there. Big brave man that he was. Is.

I knew after the good rain we'd had, the water would have collected in Bezuidenhout's field, just behind the graveyard. I'd known about that place since I was four. Harry took Sylvia and me to collect mushrooms there almost as soon as we could walk. I had a craving just then for the big, brown ones, fried in fresh butter like Harry had taught us and eaten straight away. I wanted Bart to taste them.

I tried convincing myself nothing had changed, pulling on my gumboots and squelching across the plot to the river. As usual, I tucked a plastic bag in the back pocket of my jeans. By then I'd let them out as far as I could, though I still had to use a cord and safety pin to keep them up. When I swung across the river on the rope, the wild peach tree groaned and dipped under the weight and the river snapped at my feet. Still, I made it to the other side, though that was the deepest donga my heels ever made in the river bank.

I crossed the yard of the old Papendorf place and squeezed myself through the barbed-wire fence to Bezuidenhout's field beyond. When I caught my backside on the top wire it took a full five minutes for me to right myself again. But then I felt glad I'd come. The sun was dazzling on the raindrops glued to the long blades of grass, and mushrooms were scattered across the field like planets. They rustled secretively as I put them in the packet.

I suppose I had a lot to think about; that's why I didn't hear Ivor's car pull up in the graveyard behind the field. Let alone the squeak of barbed wire as he bent to get through.

Maybe he saw me from the main road, passing. Or maybe he was there for reasons of his own. He still had his white lab coat on, so perhaps he'd come from the surgery. I only noticed him when he was standing right in front of me. Even so, I kept right on bending and picking, though by then my back was killing me.

"How can you be sure," he said at last, "that none of them are poisonous?"

"How long have I been doing this, Ivor?" I said. "I'm never a hundred per cent sure. But I've been okay till now." At last I straightened up. I held out the bag.

"Want some?"

He shook his head. "How are you?"

"I'm well." I hated having to stand like that in front of him, my thumbs digging into my back. I kicked my gumboot at a toadstool so it oozed an orange goo.

"When are you due?" Ivor asked. He hid his hands in the pockets of his lab coat as his eyes flicked expertly over me.

"First of August."

"You're seeing Grant Rebus, I suppose? Make sure he does a glycaemic and iron test, Con. You've always had a slight anaemia."

"How are *you*?" I asked.

"Well. All well."

Somewhere on the Kanonkop a baboon started barking. Ivor and I watched Jakkals prick her ears and bound to the fence. She must have run all the way around via Bloubessie Way to catch up with me.

"Connie," Ivor said, "I hope you'll let me know if you ever need anything."

"Like what?" I asked.

"I don't know." He reached out and lifted my left hand. He turned it over to examine the fresh scar just above my wrist. Then he ran his fingers up to the other one at my elbow, where the stitches had only just dissolved. So Grant Rebus had told him after all.

"If there *should* ever be anything." He rubbed his thumb across the scar then looked up at me. "Is there?"

That's how it always was with Ivor. He never asked, he just watched and waited.

But then you could say: he never asked and I never volunteered. I thought we both knew if he kept still enough, if he waited long enough, eventually I'd creep nearer. I'd feel it was safe to have a look. And then it would be too late. Snap. He'd gobble me up.

Just like now. Caught again. Or almost.

I pulled my hand away from his. "No," I told Ivor, "there's nothing I need from you."

Chapter 23

ON THE FRONT STOEP, Dr Mkhaliphi and I cup hands to peer through the big window of the bedroom that once belonged to me. Water dribbles down the glass, smudging the outlines of the two figures inside.

When I couldn't get up any more, they shifted the bed at right angles to the door. That way, whenever I opened my eyes, I'd look through the window opposite, straight out at the Kanonkop, rain or shine. I also got a good view of Harry's orchard, and the parrots when they came sweeping in.

Bart's obviously chosen to keep the bed that way.

This room was kept so tidy when I was lying here – cupboards closed, clean tray next to the bed packed with bottles of morphine and Duphalac. Princess bustling around first thing every morning: *I going to give you the bath now, Con.*

I can bath myself.

Okay, okay! Connie, I going to make the nice hot bath for you and get the new pyjamas.

What do you think I'm doing – dying?

That stopped her. I knew she wouldn't trot out all the crap other people tried pushing onto me. *Of course you're not dying. Be positive. There's always hope.*

We all going to die one day, Con, Princess said quietly, *you and me also.*

I want it to be over.

I said it partly to punish her. I hated her for being so energetic and alive. Singing or talking to herself or Marianne, who was either strapped to her back or set out on a pillow on the floor for me to see. *Don't you dare*, I told Princess the day I felt her praying over me. I didn't even open my eyes. *Don't you dare pray over me. You know what I want*, I said, *and you won't do it.*

I asked *him*, too. Ivor. He could have done it. Made a plan. Hadn't he once said I should ask him? *If there's anything I can help you with*, he said.

But when I did ask him, he said no.

Not on my conscience, he said. *The best I can do is control the discomfort.*

"She asked me to help her." On the mussed-up bed in my old room, Sylvia prods at the pink blanket Esmé crocheted when Marianne was born. Sandile sits cross-legged at her feet.

"To help her – you know," Sylvia mutters. "I couldn't do it." It's almost impossible to hear her above the rattle of rain on the roof. "I did everything else. I looked after her baby, cared for the house. I cleaned her up every day. A lot of nights I slept here next to her. I put a mattress on the floor."

And snored. And tossed and turned as if you were channelling all the bad dreams to you, not me. Getting up every two hours to go to the bathroom, fetch some water. To stand beside my bed in the dark and look down at me.

"You have been a very good sister," Sandile says.

"I hope so."

"I can tell you that you definitely have. I saw you. I saw what you did for your sister, Sylvia."

Curiosity killed the cat, I told her once. And bared my teeth. *Meow*. I smiled to show I wasn't meaning *she* was the catty one. Who could ever think that? She was just quizzy. Always wanting to know who was saying what. Trying to tug it out of you, like easing out a milk tooth.

Why didn't you tell me, Con? I'm your sister. It will be my flesh and blood too, after all. I only want to help you. We should do this together. I don't understand why you'd want to do it on your own. I don't understand why he doesn't help. "He" being Bart. She wasn't to know how many times I'd told Bart to back off.

Then she stopped asking questions and started buying things: a white Babygro on the church sale. A mobile with yellow ducks. An enormous book with *My Book of Firsts* engraved in gold across the imitation-leather cover.

Whenever I complained about life, Sylvia used to say: *everything changes*, but the rain is thundering down on the roof just like it always did, and the light is shifting in prisms through the windows as it moves on and up across the Kanonkop, which stands as it always stood.

Chapter 24

THE RAIN'S LET UP AT LAST, and a blue Ford Bantam bakkie is dawdling up Plumbago Way. Crammed onto the back are a lawn-mower, an edge trimmer, a chainsaw, two rakes, four spades, an axe and three men in blue overalls. In front, the driver's so short the reversed baseball cap he's wearing is scarcely visible over the wheel. At each house, he slows down and pulls himself taller, craning his neck to check the numbers on the gate.

In the garden shed at the back of his mother's house, Alwyn stretches and yawns from the deckchair. Nothing like a quick cat-nap. He levers himself up to stand and peers through the cracked window of the shed. The sun's coming out.

To whom it may concern ... He picks up the pad of blue note-paper he's been writing on and holds it at arm's length. *Let it be known that I* ...

Alwyn drops the writing pad on the chair. He reaches up to feel along the top shelf running the length of the shed and pulls out a bulging, knotted Checkers bag. He lays it carefully on the floor beside the chair and drops to his knees. Holding his hands palm to palm in front of him, he closes his eyes.

"Today I want to remember my friend Connie," he announces.

His nose quivers, and he cuffs it with the back of his sleeve. For a good minute he mutters under his breath, then exhales – a long sigh – and climbs back to his feet. Picking up the notepad, he settles back in the chair to continue writing.

Let it be known that I, the afourmentioned Alwyn Pretorius du Plessis van der Walt of twenty Plumbago Way, Scheepersdorp, would like to say:

<u>*Thanks.*</u>

Alwyn tears the piece of blue paper off, folds it up and places it in an envelope, licking it closed. Then he seals the envelope in a Ziploc bag and slides it into the Checkers bag.

He'd learned a lot from putting up those shelves at Toppie de Bruyn's legal practice.

No prayers, I told them. *Plant a tree if you must. Dig up some bulbs, plant them on the plot for me. But no religion or superstition.*

Alwyn swore to it. Raised his large right hand and promised me solemnly, left hand on his mother's leather Bible.

Go on, Connie, Sylvia used to say. *Forgiveness doesn't cost a thing.*

I made a promise, too. And a promise is a promise: it can't be denied because somebody else didn't keep their word.

A beam of sun sneaks through the window of the shed. It leans in to catch the top of Alwyn's bent head, and his scraggly crown blazes in the light. He looks up towards the window, almost as if he's looking at me.

I don't know I'm going to do it till I do.

Even then, it's just a split second as he scrambles to his feet. Maybe it's too quick for him to catch me, in my denim shorts and halter-neck top, grass stains on the bodice. My hair's scraped back in a pony, and there's a line of sweat across my forehead and a scar on my cheek from trimming the restios by his mother's front stoep. I don't smile. I just look into my old friend Alwyn's bulging eyes.

I can't say for sure if he sees me or not.

He certainly stands there long enough, hands dangling at his sides. And as he stares his eyes shift like a kaleidoscope: olive; muddy; luminous cat's-eye green.

Three o'clock. The clouds have disappeared, but the sky darkens briefly again. Dogs begin to bark. Almost before the clamour reaches human ears, the yellowwood has leaped into life, twitching and shuddering under attack.

Marianne doesn't let the racket from the tree put her off. In her high chair in the kitchen, she pops another Smartie into her mouth. As Bart approaches with the scissors she widens her mouth, ready to let rip again. Her tongue is parrot-green.

In the bedroom of the house a hundred metres away, Janice opens her eyes. She turns her head and a slick of drool sinks into the pillow. Her skull is throbbing. How long has she been asleep? Glancing down, she sees she's still in her bra and skirt, legs curled up on the bed. On Ivor's bedside table there's an empty whisky glass, while the duvet holds the dent of where he must have stretched out beside her as she slept.

Now he's standing at the foot of the bed. He's changed into chinos and a short-sleeved shirt, and he's glowering down at her. "Are you coming over to Sylvia's?" he asks.

Slowly, Janice raises herself to sit. She feels beside her for the neatly folded blouse. Still groggy, she fumbles for the sleeves, ready to pull it on again.

Ivor watches her threading her pale arms through the blouse. He waits until she's almost finished buttoning before he picks up his keys. Then without a word he heads for the front door.

A zing, a splutter. A whine soaring into a petrol-throated snarl. The crackle of blade meeting branches.

At the top of the driveway, the Bantam bakkie's been parked and unloaded. Already two of the overalled men are down near the river, and the third is attacking the plumbago with the edge trimmer, an oily cloud rising around him.

Dr Mkhaliphi hitches his trousers to rise from the bench. He glances up at the sun hovering over the Kanonkop, then at me.

Next thing we're both down at the back fence, watching Sylvia unhook the looped chain of the gate leading onto the plot. She's changed into a pair of old jeans and an oversized man's shirt, and she's carrying a roll of green plastic bags. Behind her, Sandile trundles a wheelbarrow loaded with secateurs, pitchfork, spade and garden trowels. Though he, too, has changed, he's still dapper in track pants, Nikes and white tee.

"Goodwill!" the undersized man with the baseball cap screeches over the jarring drone. "I want you to take fifty centimetres off. Ambition!" – to the man at the bottom of the plot – "Watch out for the tree!"

Even though the supervisor's red-faced with the effort, it's hard to believe Ambition can hear him over the hysterical parrots and gardening machinery. But Ambition – who is unusually tall – does stop and look up at the tree, cradling the chainsaw in his arms.

"Leave! *Leave!*" his boss shrills. "Don't touch that tree! Just rake up the leaves! It's just the grass and the hedge and the weeds you must bliksem! Vusi! Where's the axe? You must chop that lantana back, man. Give the axe to Vusi!"

At the back fence, Goodwill draws the trimmer slowly along the hedge. As if the machine's chewing the hedge and spitting it out again, one branch shudders to the ground. Then another.

By now the clouds have vanished and the sun's blazing back in the sky. Uproar is pelting around the valley: edge trimmers; parrots; music from the endless party at Sandile's house, where people are spilling into the yard again. Some of them wander down to lean on the bottom fence and watch the goings-on across the river.

At the top of my driveway, shadows mottle over Alwyn ambling out from under the pergola of purple bougainvillea, whistling. He's swinging a trowel in one hand and the Checkers bag from the garden shed in the other. He seems blissfully unaware of his mother, puffing up the driveway after him in her housecoat.

A couple of metres behind Esmé, the wire gate at the bottom of my driveway squeaks open, then closed again. Hands in pockets, Ivor saunters towards the pergola.

Next door, a curtain twitches at Harry Healey's lounge window. Finally, the wooden joists of his passageway begin to shudder.

It takes less than a minute for Harry to fling open his back door, motor through the orchard and across the plot, and pinpoint the cretin responsible for this latest piece of goddamn crap. "Jy! Shorty de Villiers!" Harry stoops to shove his finger in the supervisor's face. "Who told you you could come onto this land?" His powerful voice blasts loud enough for Goodwill to lower the edge trimmer from the plumbago and look questioningly at Shorty, who glances pleadingly at Sylvia. Sylvia drops the pile of duwweltjies she's just ripped up from behind the fence, wiping her forehead with the back of her hand. I recognise one of my green gardening gloves. She waves it at Goodwill and he switches the edge trimmer off.

"Uncle Harry." Sylvia trots over. "You *told* me to clean the plot up."

"*I* told you to clean the plot up? I *told* you to clean the plot up!" Harry searches behind him, but Letty's not here. Letty has made a habit of not being here lately.

"Of *course* I told you to clean the plot up. It's a bladdy health hazard!"

"You said the parrots were stealing your pecans."

"Young lady," – Harry's arm shoots out at the raucous yellow-wood – "*you* may think they're all fluffy and cute, but let me tell you. Let me tell *you*. Those birds are no better than *rats*! They're busy stripping every bladdy fruit tree for *miles*."

"I know, Uncle Harry. That's why I'm cleaning the place up," Sylvia says. "Then I'm putting it up for sale."

"Bullshit," Harry says. "Bull*shit*!"

"I'm sorry, Uncle Harry, but I really don't have a choice."

"You listen to me! You listen to me now, Sylvia West!"

"I've been told I could ask for two hundred thousand."

"*Two hun*—? Two hundred thousand *rand*? Sylvia." Harry drops his hands to his hips. He purses his lips. He looks down at his veldskoens and shakes his head. "Sylvia, Sylvia, Sylvia." His head jerks up again. "Who quoted you that? Was it Zippy Botha? That fat bastard couldn't sell rotten meat to a fly! Besides, it's unethical. It's illegal! This place is a national heritage. Do you *know*," he's yelling again, "how many protected species there are living on this piece of ground? Do you *know* what Nature Conservation would do to you if they caught you messing with them?"

Harry's last few words are drowned out by the parrots ripping out of the tree. When they've finally wheeled off towards the Kop, Sylvia says: "I need the money, Uncle Harry."

"Money, money, money!" Harry claps his forehead. "Why don't you get a decent job? Didn't I tell you to do that secretarial course at PE Technikon? Hey? Didn't I? How many times didn't I offer to pay for that? But no. Oh no-ooo. You wouldn't listen to *me*. You were waaaaay too good for *that*. What do you need so much money for, anyway? You've got a house paid off, haven't you? You've got your sister to thank for that."

"It's not just the house. It's Marianne. I—"

"What's wrong with the kid's father? Jesus. *I'll* look after her if I have to! Have I ever let you down, Sylvia? Have I?"

On the opposite bank of the river, a woman lifts her skirts to wade across from Sandile's yard. Esmé gasps as a man plunges in after her. Then another. A boy discovers the rope on the wild fig and swings over, crowing.

"Imagine what your sister would say." With his back to the river, Harry hasn't seen them yet. He steps closer to Sylvia and lowers his voice. "Your sister would be *very* disappointed in you, Sylvia. You know what I mean. No career. Nothing."

That low, mean tone that always managed to hit the mark. After all these years, Sylvia still struggles to recover from the blow. In the end, it's Esmé's shrill voice that sails into the silence.

"Look at her daughter." She tilts her head at Marianne, now clinging to Princess.

"Being brought up by …" Esmé grimaces, trying to exchange a glance only Harry's supposed to see. "Running around town with, with …"

"With what?" Sandile steps forward at last. "With who, Mrs van der Walt?" He slaps a hand on his skinny chest.

"Sandile. Esmé." Harry steps forward, raising his hands.

Dr Mkhaliphi is watching a ladybird crawl up Harry's upraised arm. Like a lone car on a highway, it putters along the freckled, sagging flesh, through the forest of long, dark hairs on his forearm towards the collar of the checked shirt. It clambers over the hillock of the purple vein beating at Harry's throat.

Dr Mkhaliphi follows the ladybird with his eyes. But he's thinking about something else, and so am I. I've finally realised what I wanted all along: I just wanted someone to listen to me.

I didn't expect whoever it was to say anything. Especially not all that crap about being positive or having hope. I just needed them to sit and hear what I was trying to tell them. And to not be afraid. Not of me. Not for me. Not of the terrible secrets I was finally going to set free. I needed them to be unshocked and ordinary and not to pretend they could fix it. Laid back. *Lacksy daisy*, as Alwyn might have said.

Once, I created that person for myself: she was a middle-aged woman with grey hair in a bun. I made her wait for me outside the x-ray cubicles and in doctors' waiting rooms after every consultation or treatment. When I came out from being examined or injected or irradiated, she'd put her knitting down to hear what had happened to me. She never offered advice or tried to cheer me up. She just concentrated on watching my story unfold in front of her. And the expression on her face was always pure and unafraid.

Dr Mkhaliphi is not a middle-aged woman with knitting. I wouldn't have thought I could get this far in my story with him. But from the start he has been listening to my tale with intent. And an expression on his face that is pure and unafraid.

Chapter 25

THE DOCTOR HAD COLD HANDS. They slid across my back, down the valleys of my armpits, prodded at my groin.

I felt like I was lying on an ice floe, thick with the gorgeous white silence of the Arctic. I kept thinking: why the hand? Why just here between palm and wrist, where Ivor used to hold me as if testing my pulse? For months my fingers had worried away at it, rolling it under my skin like a marble under velvet.

Then the others, popping up like forest fires: upper arm, armpit. Neck. Sometimes I thought it might be all the places he'd touched. Like beacons on a landscape, lighting up one by one.

The doctor's fingers slid towards my belly and stopped.

"How many weeks did you say?" Her voice came from a distance.

"Eighteen. So I'm told."

"Alright." She patted my shoulder. "You can get dressed now."

When I came out of the cubicle and sat down, she flicked on a light and the screen behind her lit up. Three large transparencies with my name scribbled at the bottom of each.

"I'd like you to look at your x-rays," the doctor said.

Islands, inlets. Dark patches of ocean. White, curving shores. I couldn't make head or tail of them. I didn't want to.

So she found a piece of paper and spread it over the file notes on the desk between us and started drawing diagrams for me, writing down numbers. Graphs and statistics. Percentages.

I watched her hands move across the desk like two giant insects sparring for paper and pen. Then I gazed down at my own hands, clenched on my lap so she couldn't see them shaking.

It's not difficult to read things upside down. I didn't even have to try. I didn't *want* to try, but some words leap out at you whether you want to see them or not. Malignancy. Cancer. Metastases.

Six storeys below, an ambulance screamed round the block, leaving in its wake the cries of vegetable hawkers and taxi guards whistling for fares. I kept wondering how long it would take me to drive home to Scheepersdorp. Two and a half hours, I reckoned. If I kept the bakkie at one-twenty and didn't stop, I might even make my house by dusk. I'd pour myself a G and T and close the door of my room. Rustle through the pile of Maggie's art books I'd heaped next to my bed. Find the Emily Dickinson with the turned-down corners.

The doctor put her pen down. Light had begun to leak from the room, and she tugged at the switch of the brass lamp on her desk. "Is it possible, Constance," she asked, "to bring a friend or family member with you? The father of the child perhaps? Someone to help you decide?"

"Decide what?"

"What kind of treatment to start you on." She sounded tired. "We need to make some important decisions. About your pregnancy and how to manage it."

I kept staring down at the streets below, trying to work out if they were the same distance as from the top of the Kop to

Harry's yard. But I heard that sentence explode like a shot, and the echo of it afterwards.

"Someone needs to help you with this decision," she tried again. "What's your relationship like with the baby's father?"

And when I still didn't answer: "I'm afraid we need to decide very soon, Constance. Connie." She said my name so softly, I finally lifted my head to look her in the eye.

She was about Harry's age, maybe older. Her hair was short and completely grey. The skin under her tired eyes sagged, but it was still possible to see a scrap of kindness there. And fear.

Maybe she was bored. Maybe she was just busy. It's possible she was trying her best to keep a line between her and me. Nobody likes taking somebody else's problems on. Especially problems like that. Maybe she wanted to make sure I didn't get too close.

I wouldn't have wanted to, anyway.

I said, "I need to tell you something, you two."

It was our first night at the house after Bart moved in. Sylvia had cooked a roast chicken for supper, and she and Bart devoured most of it while I picked away at a drumstick. By then, they knew better than to fuss over my eating. But now they both put their knives and forks down and waited for me to go on.

I'd been more moody and uncommunicative than usual for months, but I suppose they put it down to hormones and just walked wider and wider circles around me. It's not that I didn't make the effort to chat sometimes, or go down to Bart's pub for a drink. But that kind of stuff tired me out so much, I needed to be alone for a long time afterwards.

I knew I'd put this off for way too long. I kept telling myself I needed to find a time when the three of us were alone together. Sylvia was almost always with Sandile now. In the days before the BMW, we'd got used to his second-hand Toyota parked under the pergola at the kitchen door or hooting from the bottom of the driveway, always loud enough for Harry to hear. Bart and I were also pretty preoccupied with sorting out arrangements for the baby. When I finally asked him to move in, Sylvia and I cleared out the spare room between my room and the nursery, and Princess cleaned the cupboards and made up the bed. Finally, one Saturday morning, Bart parked his Peugeot in the driveway behind Sylvia's Corsa and my Isuzu bakkie, and I handed him a back-door key.

Now all that was sorted out. And I had no more excuses.

"I went to see a doctor in PE," I said that night. I was careful not to say when.

"An oncologist." I waited for that to sink in. "I went to see her about this lump on my wrist. Grant Rebus said I should."

"But what is it?" Bart kept asking when I'd finished. "What is it, what is it?"

No matter how hard I tried, the word he wanted me to say (or not say) kept sticking in my throat. Every time I tried pushing it out, I choked. It was like there was a stone lodged in my gullet. I used all the terms the doctor had taught me. The fine euphemisms: malignancy, growth, tumour. But Bart wouldn't give up. He kept going and going at me till I felt like I was either going to smack him or start crying. Eventually I got it out. I rammed the stone aside and pushed that word out into the air. The cutting, hard C of it.

"It's cancer," I said.

"How can you be sure?" Bart snapped. "Did you go for a second opinion?"

"Grant Rebus diagnosed it," I said. "The specialist in PE says it's stage four."

"But what *about* a second opinion? I mean: let's not rush into this, now."

"Bart." I put my hands flat on the table and spoke down at them. "Don't. Please. Grant suspected it right away, and Dr Peake confirmed it. She's the top oncologist in PE."

Sylvia had been too tactful to ask, but I knew what she was thinking. What they were both wondering. "It's not good," I told them. "I'm waiting till after the baby's born. Then they can try treating me." I didn't look at Bart when I said it.

The three of us must have sat there in silence for a full five minutes before Sylvia slid her hand across the table and wrapped it over my fist. Paper over rock. Then Bart laid his giant paw over hers, covering both our hands. I could feel the heat of him even through Sylvia's cool palm.

"Bart," I said, "I need you to be strong for me."

Bart stared down at the mound of hands lying on the table, like they were part of the meal, set out between the empty wine glasses and the salad and the cold, half-eaten roast chicken.

"It's okay, Con. I can take it," he said.

Chapter 26

JANICE MAKES SURE Ivor's through the front gate and well out of sight before she pulls her sandals on. Then she hurries back to the bedroom to open Ivor's bedside drawer. She knows exactly where he keeps his surgery keys. She knows where everything in this house is now. Grabbing her sunglasses, she punches in the burglar-alarm code before tripping down the hot front steps and through her front gate.

But she doesn't turn right into Plumbago Way to follow Ivor to Sylvia's place. Instead, Janice takes the opposite direction. Down Bloubessie and into Main Road she almost canters, making it in record time.

It's a quiet Saturday afternoon in Scheepersdorp. The shops are closed, and those who aren't playing golf are staying home to watch the rugby. Or they've gone down to the plot to check out what Harry Healey's up to this time.

And if anybody was there to notice her, what of it? Nobody would think it odd, Janice Shepherd popping into her husband's surgery. Anyway, no one does see her let herself in at the surgery gate.

Except me.

I stay close to her sweating skin and her shallow breathing as she opens the surgery door, as she wades through the dusty, antiseptic air of the waiting room. Janice selects another key from the bunch in her hand, pushes open the door of Ivor's room, flicks on the fluorescent light. Straight to the filing cabinet and the minute desk-drawer key she'd watched him Prestik to the back, almost as if he wanted her to know. It hasn't taken long for Janice to cotton on to the Scheepersdorp way of life. She's a natural!

If I could, I might feel shocked to see my handwriting on the grubby white envelope she finally fishes from the yellow file. But I'm too impressed with how Janice has managed this. I have never known her so devious, so intent on doing the wrong thing. And her instinct is one hundred per cent accurate. She doesn't even close the drawer before sinking into the chair behind the desk and spreading the letter open with her palms.

Dear Ivor

My handwriting, alright. Spiky, upright, spindly as the read-out on a heart monitor. It's dated two months before my death.

I know you're pissed off with me.

I wasn't keen for Grant to tell you about this. But I'm grateful for the trouble you've taken to help. I understand Dr Peake has copied you and Grant in on the treatment plans. Thanks. This can't be easy for you.

I have thought very carefully about the whole thing, and I'm satisfied I've made the right decision.

Just please don't think I'm trying to get my own back at you in some kind of sick way.

I know what you want to ask me and the honest truth is, I don't know.

At the end of the day you're just going to have to trust me to do the right thing for everyone. Whatever I do I'm not doing out of spite. It would mean a lot to me if you'd believe that.

I also hope you'll believe me when I say I want you and Janice to be happy.

Con

I remember thinking a long time about how I was going to sign that letter off. Love? Deepest affection? Your old friend? You'd think at the time I could've found something more important to obsess about than that. In the end I just left it at nothing. Ivor could think what he damn well pleased.

For a good minute, Janice stares out of the window at the plot in the distance. Harry's tiny figure is planted between those of Sandile and Esmé van der Walt. Every now and then he raises an arm and slashes it down, or stabs it at Esmé or Sandile, who's folded his arms across his chest to glare at Esmé. Sylvia and Alwyn are waiting helplessly for Harry to hit his peak. Princess has handed Marianne to Bart so she can fetch her washing in, and Bart has rocked the child to sleep in his arms.

Leaning against the back fence, Ivor observes them silently, hands in pockets. Every now and then, when he thinks nobody's watching, he sneaks a look across at the back door of his house.

"Like what?" Sandile insists. He's had enough of Harry's hectoring. He blinks down at Esmé. "Like who, Mrs Van der Walt?"

"Go on. Take it easy, man." Harry drops a hand on Sandile's shoulder. "With respect, Esmé," Harry turns to her, "Sylvia is free to be friends with whoever she wants. And she could do a lot worse than Sandile."

"Fuck you," Sylvia says. "Fuck both of you." Esmé claps a hand over her mouth, but Sylvia presses on. "I have tried my very best to do what my sister would have wanted with this place. But *neither* of you has been any help. I am *sick* of all your interfering and sabotage. You're a bunch of hypocrites. All of you." By this Sylvia means chiefly Harry and Esmé. But also most of Scheepersdorp. "Nothing I do is ever good enough for you. *Nothing.*"

Sylvia yanks off the green gardening gloves and hurls them at Harry's feet. "I am going," – she thuds up the wooden steps of the stoep, but turns to face them again at the top – "I am going to … to *donate* this land to people who need somewhere to live. Some low-cost housing. Maybe *that's* what Connie would have liked me to do."

The swing door claps shut behind her.

Dr Mkhaliphi lowers himself into the wooden rocking chair on the back stoep. Elbows on knees, he leans forward to study Alwyn loitering at the edge of the group below.

"What kind of a town is this?" he asks. It's not clear if he's talking to himself or to me.

"Jesus, Sylvia. Language." Harry glares at Sandile. "Stop smirking."

"I'm not smirking," snaps Sandile.

"Yes, you are. I paid those bloody school fees so you could find out what smirking *means*. And what does she mean she needs the money?" Harry turns on the rest of them, clustered at the bottom step of the stoep. "Have I ever let her down? Haven't I cared for her, when her mother died, and even before? And what do I get for it? Bugger all." He runs a furious, bloodshot eye across Shorty and his gardening team. "I could kill myself helping you, and you bastards would just step over my corpse," he mutters.

Beside the plumbago, Goodwill clicks restlessly at the edge trimmer's starter cord, dropping it hastily when Harry scowls at him.

"Didn't I?" Harry hollers across the valley to Letty, finally out on her back stoep. "Didn't I always look after these girls?"

* * *

168

It took me longer to tell Harry than anyone else. It was bad enough having to let him know I was pregnant, though even then he wasn't *that* upset when he realised Bart might be in with a chance. And that the odds were fifty-fifty it might finally be a boy for Harry to raise.

Every morning I'd wake up and tell myself that was the day I'd do it, but I always lost my nerve. Just the thought of dragging myself across the plot to go and find Harry in his workshop or down in the orchard felt too much for me. And how would I start the conversation? I didn't want to have to look at Harry when it dawned on him what I was trying to say.

So I ended up avoiding him. It wasn't difficult. He was always so busy with his woodwork and his golf and his orchard, and by then I had a good excuse not to move around too much.

In the end, it was Harry who came looking for me. Late one afternoon he pounded up the stairs of my back stoep waving an oddly shaped block of pine.

I was sitting in the sun reading a copy of *Carry on, Jeeves* I'd re-discovered in Maggie's collection. It was a favourite of mine, and a safe choice: I knew Jeeves and Bertie Wooster could be relied on not to fall pregnant or get cancer.

"Look, Connie!" Harry waved the block of wood at me. He was wearing his workshop apron and he smelled of sawdust and sweat. "Look here! I've started the head for the baby's rocking horse!" He flopped onto the bench opposite me.

"You see," – he held the block up – "this is going to be the snout, and these are the ears. Now I want you and Sylvia to paint the eyes, and I thought for the mane—" He stopped.

"What's wrong?" he asked.

"Uncle Harry …"

"What's it? I'll get Letty to paint the eyes, man. Her hands still shake a little, but she'll do a decent job!"

"I need to tell you something."

Harry lowered the piece of wood suspiciously. "What's the matter, Connie?"

"Uncle Harry." I turned down the corner of the page and closed the book. I smoothed my hands over my quivering belly. Of all moments, the baby had chosen that one to get a little exercise, though I was pretty used to her sharp kicks by then. I could feel Harry opposite, tensed and ready to spring. I knew his mind was already reeling through the thousand possible catastrophes he might have to deal with now. But this time I knew he would be for me, not against me. And I still can't say for sure which was harder to bear.

I told him it was too late. That there was nothing he could do.

"How was I to know?" Harry groaned into his hands. "How the hell was I supposed to know if you wouldn't tell me? It can't be too late," he insisted. "They *must* be able to do something still."

"Only once the baby's born," I said. "She doesn't need to take the rap for me."

"Connie. How can you be so stubborn …" Harry lifted his head. "How do you know it's a she?"

I went and sat next to him, then. Because more often than not that's how it is. At the same time as you're drawing your sword to face down whatever you've got to face alone, you're having to say to those watching helplessly beside you: take courage. Be brave.

"Once she's born, I can do what they want, and I need your help with that, Uncle Harry," I said. "I know you'll help me then."

"Haven't I always done that, Connie?" he sighed.

Chapter 27

"WHAT THE HELL ARE you all standing around for?" Harry explodes. He's hoping Sylvia can hear from inside. "Get back to work! I'm not paying you bastards to stand around doing nothing, you know!"

Sandile shakes his head. He knows better than to take on Harry now. Besides, Sylvia has begged him not to interfere. He picks up the handles of the wheelbarrow and trundles it off, as far from Harry as possible.

"Go on," Harry barks at Shorty de Villiers. He's found a switch from the plumbago hedge, and he whips it against his leg as he orders, "Get on with it. We haven't got all day."

Shorty nods at Goodwill. Within seconds, the edge trimmer is roaring over the plumbago again. At the bottom of the plot, Vusi raises the axe to the lantana, and Ambition, having dumped the chainsaw, picks up his rake again. Down at the river bank, Alwyn rips out a clump of duwweltjies. Sandile trundles the wheelbarrow past, muttering, and Alwyn looks towards Harry and laughs.

Even some of the parrots have ventured back to the yellow-wood. A small brave group has discovered some fruit on the crown of the tree, and they twist their green necks to get to it, ignoring the disruptions below.

"For I was a stranger," Dr Mkhaliphi mutters. He's standing beside me at the edge of the stoep, swaying a little. For a moment it seems he might topple over. "I was a stranger and ye took me not in: naked, and ye clothed me not: sick, and in prison, and ye visited me not." He pauses to watch Alwyn tug at another weed. "I have always known—" Dr Mkhaliphi stops. He glares at me.

"I am a stranger to this town," he repeats, and slumps onto the top step of the stoep. He pulls out a white handkerchief from his breast pocket and mops his face. In the weakening sun, his shaved skull gleams, ochre yellows and swirling oranges.

"Are you coming down to the tree?" I ask.

"Just now," he says, and his eyelids droop.

I leave him there, head nodding onto his chest. He's back in torn shirt-sleeves and no tie, and the wound on his chest is pulsing again.

If you were looking down at them from the crown of the tree, eight metres up, their limbs would seem to be whirling round their oval heads. The tall man, Ambition, raking leaves. Goodwill aiming the edge trimmer at the plumbago like a rifle. Vusi hacking at the lantana. Alwyn kneeling to dig, while Sandile wheels the barrow towards another patch of blackjacks and duwweltjies.

"Watch out!" From the top fence, Harry shakes his plumbago switch at Ambition, even though he's raking a good three metres from the yellowwood. "Don't touch that tree!" Harry thunders. "It's a *Podocarpus henkelii*! Leave it alone, man. Leave it alone!"

The longer Sylvia stays indoors, the louder Harry becomes. He's battling, now, against the parrots, which have suddenly shrieked up from the yellowwood. For over a minute they wheel around the tree, batting furious wings before flying off again. One bird takes longer to follow the flock, flapping frantically around the crown of the yellowwood with almost-human cries. It's as if it's trying to tell us something. Esmé, on her way down the path with more rolls of green plastic bags, hesitates at the parrots' hullabaloo. Only Bart remains on the stoep, Marianne fast asleep in his arms. Beneath her ruddy cheek, a small patch of drool soaks into his shirt.

Let's go back to the top of the tree. Look at Ambition raking below, head swivelling and bobbing as his arms pull and push. For some time he's been working steadily. But when the parrots flare up and circle the tree with their blood-curdling screams, Ambition stops to tilt his head back. He stares up at the yellowwood, his face a still pond. Now someone has tossed a pebble in. Rings within rings, his face ripples open, wider and wider. The speechless O of his mouth and eyes. The rake drops to the ground. Ambition's mouth expands. He wants to shout. But no sound emerges.

Slowly he edges away from the tree. When he reaches the path, he turns his back on the yellowwood and breaks into a trot. Then a run. Up the embankment, through the back gate he sprints, right up onto the stoep, two steps at a time. He has finally found his voice. And on hearing it, Sandile, Harry, Goodwill, Shorty and Vusi all freeze. They stare at Ambition, waving at them from the stoep, gesturing at the tree. Goodwill, Shorty and Vusi edge towards the path, though Harry narrows his eyes and makes a point of standing his ground, casually slapping the plumbago switch against his trouser leg. Beside the river, Sandile watches, waiting for Harry to make the first move. And when he does, finally striding off towards the back gate, Sandile forces himself into a tense amble. When he reaches the back fence, he clears it in one spectacular leap, dreadlocks spinning.

The women and the boy from across the river have no such

qualms. On hearing Ambition's cry, four whirring sets of arms and legs shatter through ant heaps and thorn bushes. One stout woman stumbles into a wheelbarrow, the other crunches her bare foot into a patch of uprooted duwweltjies. But they thunder on towards the back gate. In one last push they land in a heap on the stoep.

Only Alwyn doesn't budge. He alone wanders in the opposite direction to the others, down towards the yellowwood, where he tilts his head to look up.

At the far end of my driveway, Ivor pauses before opening the gate onto Plumbago Way. He stops to listen. *Now* what are they going on about? He can't quite hear.

"Inyoka!" Ambition screams again, pointing at the yellowwood.

At last the screen door squeaks open. Sylvia appears in the doorway, dirty-faced, red-eyed. From behind her, Princess shuffles out in slippers, right to the edge of the stoep. She screws her eyes up to stare at the yellowwood.

"Jay-sus," shudders Princess.

Mesmerised, they all watch a slim shadow sway up from the top branch of the tree. Three or four times it swings gently back and forth, as if it's trying to grip the sky. Then it clasps at a green bough and melts back again.

The plumbago on the fence, already bent for the coup de grâce, eases back into place. A spider scurries to the centre of its web in the acacia tree. The *Dietes grandiflora* on the river bank shiver and grow still. In the soft clay beside them a spade trembles, abandoned. And the river prances on.

On the eighteenth hole of the Scheepersdorp golf course, Toppie de Bruyn swings a five iron and hooks the ball into the rough. He doesn't care any more. He's already up to a hundred and ten. Harry Healey never arrived for golf this afternoon. For once, Toppie had hoped to better his score without awkward legal questions as he was about to tee off, or comments about his lousy choice of clubs. Never mind. It will all feel alright after a few Klippies and Cokes. The others will rib him about his lousy golf. Maybe after a few toots they can call Harry up on the blower. Persuade him to drive over in his golf cart.

Though Toppie can't quite make up his mind whether he *wants* Harry to come over or not. Harry's been no fun since he lost the mayoral election.

Across the valley, the smell of roast boerewors and lamb ribbetjies singes the air. The first braais of summer. In the next valley, the *thump*, *thump*, *thump* of the beat from the township starts up.

Janice is walking up Main Road, slower than she did earlier today. The trampled jacaranda flowers cling to her white sandals, and her head leans forward on her long neck to watch each swell and crack of the pavement.

At the corner of Plumbago and Bloubessie, she slows down, hesitating before deciding to turn right into Bloubessie Way.

Which is just as well, as it allows her to catch sight of her husband in the distance, approaching from the far end of Plumbago Way.

So he has come looking for her. I read somewhere that the French say there is one who kisses and one who offers the cheek. Until now, Ivor has only offered Janice the cheek. But some uneasy impulse has brought him looking for her this late afternoon. He's not normally prone to feelings like this. But it's as well for him, this time, to follow his instinct.

He kissed *me*. I didn't even offer my cheek. Not in any obvious way. Not in a way anyone other than he would have understood. He sat waiting till he caught me. And when he caught me he kissed my fingernails with the dirt caked underneath.

Sweating up the Kanonkop, face pale, his thin shadow flitting at my heels. Toiling silently behind me but never once refusing to go up when we asked him. Me and Alwyn either end, showing him the way. Safe in the middle. Always better when Alwyn was there – Alwyn with his big stick to scare off the snakes. But he grew brave enough to go without Alwyn, eventually. For a while, I was good enough.

More than good enough. Better.

Without speaking, Ivor and Janice have fallen into step. Neither of them knows where they're headed. But they allow themselves to be pulled up, under the long line of jacarandas, to the top of Plumbago Way.

Along both sides of the road, curtains are being inched aside. No need to hear what they're saying to guess what's going on between Dr Shepherd and his wife.

Back and forth like tennis balls *pok-pokking* over the nets at the Scheepersdorp Tennis Club. A swift serve: "Can you not just talk to me?" A volley, a sneaky backhand, a long rally: "How can I start sorting things out if I don't know what's going on in your head? If I don't know the truth?" In her own way, Janice has never been one to give up easily. Back and forth they go. "All I want to know," she says, "all I'm asking is: what really went on between you and her?"

Head down, Ivor walks on. It's as if there's something fascinating or repellent on the tips of his polished brown shoes. He knows how many sets of eyes are lined up over kitchen sinks and behind lounge windows to watch. But he's almost too tired to care.

"You say it was over between you and Connie by the time we met," Janice tries again. Unlike their walk home from the surgery, this time *she's* the one having to trot to keep up with *him*.

"It was," Ivor says.

"Then why—"

"God. Why do we have to go over this *again*?" He lifts his cold gaze to her face.

Poor Janice. She has stumbled into one of those deep, blind places you should avoid at all costs. The bottom of a cave, the dead-end road. You asked for it. You insisted on coming this far. You refused to pretend it wasn't there, that it would never happen to *you*. And here you are at last. Here is what comes of your endless questioning.

This is what you wanted, isn't it? Don't turn away now. Turning away is no longer an option.

Even if Janice doesn't look, even if she suddenly decides she doesn't want to hear the truth after all, it's too late. Because by now Ivor doesn't need to say another word for Janice to know her suspicions have been right all along. In the middle of the pavement, they stop and stare at each other.

The fine, colourless hairs on Janice's freckled arms bristle. The thing that has slept between them for so long is finally beginning to shudder and sit up.

Puddles of light have started to leak out of the kitchen windows onto the dusky pavements. They are trembling on the slasto and concrete of the shadowy Scheepersdorp yards. Like minnows, glances dart across to where Janice and Ivor stand – so visible to the whole road! – facing each other.

Who, everyone is wondering, will make the first move?

"For crying out loud!" Harry would have said if he'd seen Ivor slip through the swing doors of the ward after the others had all left. "For crying in a bucket!" He'd heard somebody say that in an American movie once. "What the hell is *he* doing here now?"

I heard Ivor's shoes first: squeaking across the parquet of the Scheepersdorp Nursing Home towards my bed. He thought I hadn't seen him earlier, peering through the open door of the ward. I knew he was waiting for the others to leave. Letty and Sylvia and Esmé were still crowded round my bed, handing Marianne around. As soon as she had the child in her arms, Esmé started to cry and Letty had to take her outside. Sylvia sat on the edge of the bed rocking Marianne. She kept stroking her nose or her eyebrows, as if that would give her a better idea who the baby looked like.

"She's got Bart's nose," Sylvia said. She didn't sound convinced.

When I looked up past her, I saw Ivor peering through the door again, fringe flopping over his eyes. I almost laughed out loud. Fortunately, Sylvia's back was turned to him, and she was too busy checking out the baby to notice anything else.

By the time they'd all left, Marianne was asleep and tucked up in the crib next to me, ready for the nurse to fetch her. Bart had spent an hour there already, but he'd had to get off to the pub before six. Alwyn couldn't get out of bed by then, and Harry didn't like hospitals at the best of times. And under these circumstances … I knew he was so churned up about what was happening to me, he couldn't bear to look at me. In the end *I'd* have to be the one visiting *him*. So Ivor would have known the coast was clear.

I was lying on my side with my back to the door and the child in the crib, so at first he might have hoped I was asleep. When I heard his footsteps – that familiar, hurried tread – I kept my eyes shut, though I could sense him standing beside the bed. Then I heard the shuffle of the crib blankets being pulled back and the baby being lifted.

He carried her over to the window, where his profile was perfectly outlined against the light. The expression on his face when he looked down at her: I'd say it was clinical. Like he was thinking hard before making a tricky diagnosis.

He stared at her for at least five minutes, then brought her back again. He took his time tucking her into the crib, making sure all the blankets were tight around her and she was lying comfortably on her back. By that time, I'd turned round to watch.

"Congratulations," he said when he'd finished. He stood with his hands behind his back. "What are you calling her?"

"Marianne. Marianne Constance West."

"My mother's second name was Marianne."

"Was it?" I tried to sound surprised. Obviously Ivor hadn't realised how many books Maggie signed in her full name.

We watched Marianne shift her head from side to side on the stretched cotton sheet.

"She's warming up," I said. "I hope the nurse is coming soon."

"I'll call her," Ivor said, but he stayed where he was.

"Connie, I have to ask. Is there any chance that she …" He rocked forward on his toes. "That we …" He stopped.

I felt a terrible weariness open up and swallow me. The anaesthetic, the excitement, the blur of attention, even the thin edge of hope that appeared every now and then: all evaporated and I was worn down to the bone. My tongue and mouth were exhausted from acting for the rest of me, the endless explaining. I felt like I never wanted to speak again. For the first time, closing my eyes and sleeping forever didn't seem the terrible thing everyone else made it out to be.

"Ivor. I'm really tired," I said.

I watched him reach down and offer his pinky finger to the baby, and her fingers curl slowly over it. It reminded me of a chameleon testing a branch with its paw.

"She's strong enough," said Ivor at last.

"Like her mother," I said.

When Ivor spoke again he was talking to Marianne.

"I hope," he said, letting her gnaw his finger, "that you are."

Chapter 28

"Come along, my darling. Come along." Alwyn shakes a hessian sack open under the yellowwood. Then he lifts a long, hooked stick and manoeuvres it gently up, barely stirring the top branches of the tree. Alwyn's eyes bulge. His mouth purses with concentration. Nobody can see what he's aiming for. There's not the slightest rustle or tremble, and the yellowwood stands its ground, impervious and still. But Alwyn has a sixth sense about these things. He holds the stick steady, ignoring the crowd on the stoep behind him and their restlessness. He pays no mind to the madly panicking parrots now circling Harry's pecan-nut trees.

At last, olive green and indolent, a branch separates from a bough at the crown of the tree. For a second it halts, coolly indifferent to the furore of parrots. Then it rears slowly up and sways towards the stick.

Finally she shows herself. As if she's been waiting all this time, but only for Alwyn's sure hands.

I could watch forever the way her daggered head eases out of the nest of needles. For a few seconds she lifts her enormous diamond eyes, moist and unblinking. She gazes down at them all: Harry, Esmé, Sylvia, Sandile. Bart and Marianne. Princess in her slippers. Ambition and Goodwill and Shorty and Vusi.

In her slim, green silence she drinks it all in: the Kanonkop, the plot, the parrots, the soundless people below. Then she tips her head forward and pours onto the hooked stick like honey.

Gently, Alwyn lowers the stick to the ground to angle it at the open mouth of the mealie sack. Harry, the only one willing to hold the bag, is wearing Sylvia's gardening gloves as well as a couple of green plastic bags he's wrapped round his arms – but he still stands as far back as he can while the stick steers towards the sack. With one arm, Alwyn edges the stick in. With the other, he prods lightly with a pitchfork.

Harry hopes Sylvia is watching. The things he does for her!

As soon as she's glided safely in, Harry knots the two corners of the sack together. Then Alwyn knots them again. He places the bulging bag in the wheelbarrow and pushes it tenderly into the last bit of sun.

Beside me, Dr Mkhaliphi yawns and sits up. Marianne lifts her head from Bart's chest and removes her thumb from her mouth. She opens her eyes and looks directly at us. Tears have tracked down her dirty cheeks and the fine wide space of her forehead is open for all to see.

"I cannot see that she looks much like you," Dr Mkhaliphi says.

"She's got my colouring," I say. And she has: blonde hair, pale cheeks. That dip of sallow colour at the base of her chin and that tip of pink on her nose.

"But she has blue eyes," Dr Mkhaliphi says. "Like Bart."

I hold his gaze.

"Yes," I say coolly, "like Bart."

*　*　*

Sylvia stood in my doorway holding Marianne. She was asking what fertiliser to use on the plum tree outside my window. She knew how much I loved the fruit, and she was doing her level best to look after it for me. Suddenly she looked down at the bundle in her arms.

"She's smiling!" Sylvia said.

"Must be wind." I didn't know a lot about babies, but I'd read about that somewhere.

"No, look Con, she's definitely smiling. Look!" Before I could stop her, Sylvia plumped the baby in my arms. I had a couple of cushions propped up behind me but I was barely sitting up. Even though my last chemo had been four days before, I was still nauseous and shivering.

"Look there," Sylvia squealed, "there it is: Marianne's first smile! We can write it in the book!"

I looked down at the hot, fleshy package in my arms. For once, she wasn't crying. Her fingers were sticking out of the blanket like mouse claws and she pursed her bottom lip out and blew spit bubbles at me. She seemed a little squint. One eye was vaguely focused on Sylvia, while the other wandered around the ceiling. Then, as I watched, both eyes snapped into sync again. She looked straight up at me and beamed.

Sure enough, at the same time a tiny dent appeared in each of her cheeks.

"Connie, don't tell me she's not smiling at you now."

"It's wind." I pushed the baby back at Sylvia, almost dropping her. "Her nappy needs changing."

Then I lay back and drew my arm over my eyes. From a long way away I heard a gulp, then a steadily upsurging howl – actually it was more like a bray. It took me a few seconds to realise the noise was coming from me.

Once I'd started I couldn't stop. Trouble was, I set the baby off too. Poor Sylvia. She couldn't think what to do first. She ran to the door but collided with Bart, who'd just strolled in with a Castle to sit with me. Sylvia couldn't make up her mind if she should give the baby to Bart and stay with me, or run and look for Princess. But Bart must have taken control, because through all the noise and commotion I eventually heard Sylvia's bare feet pounding off down the passageway and Marianne's wail growing fainter and fainter.

"Go away," I told Bart. But he knew I didn't want him to. I kept my arm over my eyes. I didn't want to see on his face how I'd finally caved in and let them all down. Maybe I told him that through all the crying. I can't remember.

"Oh," I heard Bart say. It wasn't so much a word as a groan. His knees banged down on the wooden floor beside my bed.

For a long time he knelt there without talking. Even though there was nothing between the hard floor and his knees, he still had to lean down to get his face level with mine. He put the Castle down on the floor next to him, and stroked my hair without saying a word. When I wiped my face with the back of my hand, I felt something being pushed into my palm. A crumpled paper serviette with *Bart's Pub and Grill* printed on the corner. It looked like it had already been used. But I blew my nose on it and lay back on the pillow at last. I closed my eyes.

I don't know how much later it was that I heard Bart shift back and stagger up from his knees to stand. The floorboards creaked and the bedroom door clicked shut behind him. By now the baby's voice had become a low, distant whine, like the hum of a sewing machine. Above it, Bart's footsteps faded off down the passageway.

Bit by bit, my chest stopped shuddering. I blew my nose on the serviette one last time and felt myself drifting off. I felt emptied of whatever had been building up in me. Almost, one might say, at peace. Possibly just numbed. I was almost asleep when the door clicked open again.

His arms were so crammed you could barely see his wild curls above the branches of buchu and plumbago and arum lilies from the river bank. There were even some nasturtiums from the gutters at the kitchen door, and two mildewed roses he must have stolen from Janice's back yard.

Until then, I'd still been quite sceptical about how much attention Bart paid when I took him down to the plot. But every plant I ever showed him was in that bunch, plus a half-opened bobbejaantjie, which should rightly have been left to flower.

He'd found a tin bucket in the shed and there was a trail of water running from the passage all the way to my bed. Bart placed the bucket opposite the bed where I could see it best, and with his enormous hands plonked the branches and flowers into it. Then he sat down on the floor next to me again – he was too big to perch on the bed – and I let him stroke my hair until I fell asleep, deeply this time.

When I woke two hours later, he was still there. The buchu and nasturtium fragrance flooded the room, and shadows were pooling around Bart's shoulders and the three empty cans of Castle on the floor beside him.

Chapter 29

"THE FACT IS, JANICE," – Ivor closes his fingers around her wrist – "the fact is I chose *you*."

The two of them, after arguing to the top of Plumbago Way, have turned and bickered their way down again, right into the open gate of number twenty-two. They're so busy scoring points that neither wonders why they're climbing the driveway to Connie West's back yard.

Does Janice even realise where they're headed? Ivor may have remembered Sylvia's drinks invitation, but he's not keen to mention the West sisters right now.

Perhaps it's the sudden silence on the plot, after all the chaos, that pulls Janice in. *What are they getting up to this time? These people.* She's never been able to see how quizzy she is, and how it lands her in situations she should probably avoid.

Janice and Ivor only stop when they reach the pergola at the top of the driveway where the bougainvillea tumbles down.

"I asked you to marry me," Ivor says. "I *did* marry you."

For the moment, both of them ignore the explosion of applause – whistles, shrills, clapping – from the back yard, where Alwyn has finally coaxed the snake into the hessian bag.

"And I married you." When Janice finally speaks, her voice is thin and remote.

"Yes," says Ivor politely. "Thank you."

Poor Janice. She can't help herself. Almost without her permission, her fingers have begun to squeeze his. Such a slight return of pressure, he might not recognise (although he does, distinctly) that she's trying to tell him something.

Things won't ever again be as fresh and clear for Janice as they were on her wedding day. From this day forth there will be questions. Row after row they spring to attention, beside and behind her. For the rest of her marriage Janice will have to learn to look away.

"Do you know how hard they're trying for a baby?" Sylvia asked. It was five months after the wedding. "They've been trying since even before they got married. Janice says she wants three."

"I know. She told me."

Sylvia frowned. "Did she? That's surprising. I would have thought ..."

"That was before she found out," I said. "But Janice is different. She doesn't hold things against people unless she really has to."

"Hold things against people?" Sylvia raised her eyebrows. "I would have thought it would be the other way round."

"Meaning her and Ivor? Oh, I don't know." Sometimes I liked telling Sylvia things, sometimes I didn't. Too often she made the mistake of being just too damn eager to know. That always shut me down.

But after a while I asked, "What are they doing? About the baby?"

"All sorts: fertility experts, drugs, ovulation tests."

"She told you all that?"

"Yes." Sylvia looked puzzled. "She seems to have taken me on. I don't really understand it."

"Sylvia," I laughed, "*anyone* can understand it. You listen to her. You look as if you care. You probably *do* care. Of course she's going to confide in you. Also, she probably thinks you don't tell anyone else."

"Well, I don't." Sylvia pursed her lips primly.

"Except me."

"Well, yes." Now she laughed with me. "I don't know, Connie. You *are* naughty. No matter how much I tell myself I'm not going to tell you, I end up doing it. And I'm not like that with anyone else."

"We *are* sisters," I said dryly.

"Yes." I know she'd have liked to hug me. But she settled for putting a hand on my arm instead.

"Con?" She rested her hand there for a minute.

"Mmm?"

"I need to ask," she started.

When Sylvia lowered her voice like that I always had to listen carefully. I knew it was going to be one of those rare occasions when she was going to stick to her guns.

"What are your plans for this baby?"

"Sylvia." I hesitated. She didn't deserve to be snapped at. To be honest, I was touched. And I knew it took courage to ask. "You don't need to worry," I told her. "Bart and I are sorting it out. He's going to help with maintenance, and we're getting Princess to come in full time." I even managed to squeeze her hand. "You really don't need to worry."

Sylvia thought this over. "I'm surprised at Bart," she murmured eventually. "I would have thought he'd be the kind of man who'd at least offer to move in and help you with the baby."

"He did," I said, equally casually. "And I said no."

187

She needed to think about that one, too. You could almost feel her tiptoeing through the conversation. She was so afraid of choosing the wrong door and getting it slammed in her face. "Well," she said at last, slowly, "it's probably a very good thing not to rush into anything."

"That's how I see it."

"And he can still see his child all the time."

"Absolutely. We are going to be civilised about this."

"I would expect nothing less of you and Bart."

I could almost be proud of myself, the way she looked at me.

Janice thought no one would see her, feeling her way across the overgrown path from their house to my back fence. Surely she'd been in Scheepersdorp long enough to know nothing goes unnoticed here?

Secretly, I was impressed. I knew how scary it must have been for her to try to make her way, not only to my house, but via the plot. That path hadn't been used for a good ten months and had grown blurred and tangled with plants.

One thing Janice wouldn't have expected was for me to be awake at that ungodly hour. Much less looking out of my kitchen window. But I'd slept most of the day, listening to the others opening curtains and cooking meals and going in and out to work. Now they were asleep and I was wide awake. I'd been doing that most nights – enjoying the silence of Marianne napping a few hours at a time. I'd drift through the house, picking up Bart and Sylvia's jerseys and newspapers and supper plates, figuring out what they'd eaten, piecing together the day they'd had while I'd slept.

I didn't switch on the kitchen lights. There was enough moonlight for me to see what I needed to. Sylvia was a very light sleeper and I didn't want her coming through to ask if I was okay again. Bart, on the other hand, slept like a log. His snores didn't seem to bother anyone else, but I could hear him even from the far end of the house.

At the kitchen window, I stared out at the light-hemmed clouds curling over the Kop. The yellowwood leaves were streaked with silver and the khaki bush shuddered as something burrowed at its roots. A torch was bobbing across the plot towards my back gate, where the outside light had been considerately switched on.

She was in her blue tracksuit and takkies, her hair scraped back in a pony. Stepping through shrubbery and shadows, hooking back branches, her face shone pale enough for me to make out the terror and relief once she made it to our back gate. She looped the wire catch off the wooden stump, flicked off her torch and walked – already more confident – towards the light shining at the back of Princess's flat.

"In," I heard Princess call. The door eased open and I saw a long slice of light. There was a brief glimpse of Princess, barefoot in her church clothes, copper bangles glinting on her ankles. Then the door swung shut again.

If I craned my neck I could make out their shadows spreading across the curtains of Princess's high window. But I couldn't hear what they were saying. Just the low drone of Princess's voice and a couple of short shrill responses from Janice.

I heard Marianne stir and whimper in her cot in Sylvia's room. From her basket near the back door, Jakkals twitched her ears.

Half an hour later, Princess's door creaked open again and Janice's figure appeared briefly in the doorway. The moon was blanketed by a cloud, and in the sudden darkness her torch flicked on again. Hiding myself behind the half-drawn kitchen curtain, I heard the back gate creak open and thud shut. Footsteps rustled and faded down the path.

It was Princess who kept me there. She stood in her doorway, skinny arms folded, watching Janice's torch bump back across the plot. Then, although she had no way of knowing I was there, she turned and spent a full minute staring at the kitchen window where I stood.

"I am praying for you, Connie," Janice said.

"I am praying for you, too, Janice."

You could see she didn't know how to take that. Poor Janice. No matter how hard she tried, her red cheeks always gave her away. "Thank you," she said uncertainly.

It had taken courage, I'll give her that. You could see she'd thought a lot about what to wear – smart or casual? – for what everyone knew would be her last visit to my house. I don't even know if Ivor knew she was there that day, but she'd thought about it long enough to call ahead. And to bake a batch of scones.

I didn't hate her. She was doing what she thought right. We hadn't spoken for months – ever since my bump became common knowledge in Scheepersdorp. If we met in the shops or passed each other in the street, we'd merely nod to each other and walk on.

I wonder who told her about my illness. Whose dinner party or tea or urgent phone call passed on that last, delicious morsel of news? I wonder how long they all took to taste and chew and swallow it.

When my doorbell rang at exactly ten a.m., Princess had just strapped Marianne to her back. I could hear Janice exclaiming in the high, sweet voice people so often use for babies, then Marianne grizzling as they walked down the passageway. The smell of scones wafted ahead of them to where I sat on the back stoep in the sun.

"Connie. Look." We'd got through all the polite stuff. Now Janice leaned forward in her chair. She galloped helter-skelter at the words, all caution thrown to the wind again. This was more like it. I preferred it when people got down to the nitty-gritty.

"Please don't take this the wrong way," Janice said, "but they have a faith-healing on Thursdays at our church." She had her hands clasped over her knees and kept fiddling with her wedding ring. "What we do is we pray for people who are ill. We're praying for Alwyn at the moment." She paused. "Esmé comes along, too."

As if that would clinch it for me.

"What I mean is, Connie, if you ever felt like—" Janice stopped. I raised my eyes to gaze past her at the plot. The sun was sliding over the rooftops, spilling onto my back stoep. Light slipped around Janice's tall silhouette and moved on to find me, hunched in the rocking chair in my sagging tracksuit and sheepskin slippers. I let it sink into me till it felt like the outlines of my body were blurred and my bones were starting to dissolve.

"If you ever felt like coming along," Janice gabbled, "we lay healing hands on people. It can't do any harm. After all. You've got nothing to lose." Her teacup rattled back into its saucer.

I wondered how many prayer sessions Janice had attended for herself and how she managed to keep believing in them, or in Princess and her medicine and her prayers, or in whatever desperate measure next caught her eye. I couldn't blame her. In my own way, I understood how bloody it was to finally let go of hope.

"You're right." I smacked my hands on the arms of my chair and started to laugh. "I have absolutely *nothing* to lose."

Janice's mouth pursed up in horror. For a moment she looked as if she might cry. I was in no mood for helping her out, but I wished she'd look behind her. The tips of the yellowwood branches were licking at the morning sun. Green shoots exploded in slow motion from the branches of the acacia near the river. A flock of white-eyes was tackling the plumbago blossoms and the hedge shivered like a dog being scratched behind the ears.

Before my eyes, brown was fading to green, from the valley up the neck of the Kanonkop. I knew that if you stood under the red rock at the top of the Kop you'd be able to watch the river capering through the plot, down through Scheepersdorp to the bridge and beyond.

"I didn't mean it that way," Janice said.

I turned to look at her. There was a smear of strawberry jam at the corner of her mouth. It was just a shade or two darker than the blush spreading over her cheeks. On the table between us, butter pooled into the centres of the scones she'd brought. I hadn't touched one.

"What did you say?" I asked.

I went into Sylvia's bedroom looking for dagga that day. Up until three weeks before, I'd never done anything like that, but I'd been complaining about nausea so much, and a few people had said I should try it. In the end I asked Sylvia to get me some.

I never found out where she got it, or how she managed to source it so quickly. All I know is Wednesday morning I put my order in, and by Wednesday evening, Sylvia and I were in the lounge having our first spliff. At least, it was the first time for me. The way Sylvia rolled and handled that zol didn't strike me as the work of an amateur.

"Did it help with the nausea?" Bart asked.

"I'm not sure," I said. "It certainly took my mind off it."

And that's why I went scrabbling through Sylvia's chest of drawers that day: I needed to take my mind off things. I was alone in the house. Sylvia and Bart were at work and Princess had taken Marianne down to the plot to kick in the sun for a bit.

Princess thought I was sleeping, but even though I was still in bed I couldn't get comfortable. I felt restless and exhausted at the same time.

I told myself it was fine to be by myself, but it wasn't true. It was one of those times I didn't enjoy the loneliness. I didn't feel like waiting till Bart or Princess came back; I needed something to push the time forward. Or take it completely away. And as Janice so rightly said: what did I have to lose?

I found the tin in Sylvia's top drawer, tangled in among size L panties and 38DD bras. She didn't even try to hide the stuff away. When I opened the lid, I saw three joints already neatly rolled. I was about to shut the drawer when I saw the *Book of Firsts* lying right at the back. I pulled it out and carried it over with the tin to Sylvia's bed.

I made sure the door was closed before I lit up and took a deep draw. Then I sat back and started paging through the book.

The first few pages had spaces for name and date of birth and weight and eye colour. Sylvia had filled in every detail neatly. On page two it had *First Smile*, and Sylvia had written: *11th September 1994: I smiled at my mommy while she was talking to Auntie Sylvia.*

I told myself I felt even more nauseous after that, so I took another drag. I'd say this time it helped significantly. I turned the page to first haircut, first tooth (both blank), and then to page four, headed: *Looks Like.* In the dotted lines underneath, Sylvia had filled in: *Mommy's nose, Daddy's blue eyes.* I flipped through to the end of the book, where there were two pages for *My First Day of School.* I was beginning to feel carefree about the whole thing. The tightly wound thread in my chest was almost completely unreeled, and it struck me suddenly that it was not thread, but broad, silky ribbon with a crimson sheen. As I looked down at the book, the pages melted and pushed purple satin and flowers and emerald-green birds with wide beaks up at me. The ribbon surged around them, plaiting them together. I realised I had something immensely important to say. A message to be passed on only through me.

I put the zol down carefully on the saucer I'd remembered to bring along. Then I found my way perfectly easily to Sylvia's desk. I placed the *Book of Firsts* on top of the desk, and stretched out my hand. Miraculously, a pen slid into it.

It would be the first time the world had ever heard this extraordinary thing. It was an insight to be preserved for eternity. I flipped over to the next clean page of the book and wrote in block letters:

She has her Aunt Sylvia's hair. And her dimples and her smile.

Chapter 30

FIVE O'CLOCK. As if someone's tipped a jug of ink into the sky, shadows begin to deepen under the yellowwood and the other plants, and under the figures returning to the plot.

It's taken some persuading to get everyone down here again. Only once Alwyn has trundled the wheelbarrow all the way down the long driveway, placed the brown sack in a tin trunk punched with holes in the back of his bakkie, locked the trunk and the bakkie, and parked the bakkie at the far end of the road, are Ambition and Goodwill and Vusi willing to set foot on the plot once more.

In fact, Esmé has joined the three of them in spending some time trying to persuade Alwyn to let Ambition and Goodwill beat the sack with hammers and spades until it's stained red and no longer thrashes and bulges. But Alwyn won't be budged. He tells them the snake will be taken somewhere safe. And when he says it – when his eyes flatten to that dirty olive green and his jaw grinds away behind his pock-marked cheeks – even Esmé knows there will be no arguing with him.

Bags of grass cuttings and leaves are scattered around the plot. The edge trimmer has finally been switched off. For the time being, the parrots have flown away. Now there is only the murmur of voices, the hiss and scrape of leaves being raked into piles as the last rays of sun stroke the Kanonkop.

Harry has been circling nearer and nearer to Sylvia. He hasn't said a word yet about her and Sandile pulling out the Port Jackson saplings near his back fence. For years, the birds have been seeding them there, and for years I'd been pulling them out. As soon as Harry saw me getting rid of them, he decided he needed a line of Port Jacksons as a windbreak for his place. In the end I used to weed them out on Saturday afternoons when Harry was at golf. He knew exactly what I was doing, but he pretended not to notice. And I pretended not to notice him not noticing.

"Not like that. Stupid bastard." Harry flicks his plumbago switch in Shorty's direction. He hovers closer to Sylvia again. It's like watching a hawk circle a parrot. Or a dove. He's got one hand behind his back and with the other he slashes the plumbago stick down on the hedge. Every now and then he brings the stick down extra hard. It's like a waltz: slash, slash, SMACK, slash, slash, SMACK.

Side by side, Sylvia and Sandile dig and pull, pretending not to notice Harry orbiting. With his shirt off and neatly folded on the stoep, Sandile's skinny chest is cross-hatched with scratch marks and sweat. Before he pulls each sapling out, he loosens the roots with a pitchfork.

Sylvia just uses her hands, kneeling in front of each tree to dig with bare fingers and slacken the soil. Then she hauls the tree out in one pull. By now, her hair's tumbling out of her thick ponytail and the back of her tee-shirt is dark with sweat.

"So are you not talking to me now?" Harry finally stops behind Sylvia. Slash, slash, SMACK – he whips the switch at a large aloe, barely missing its flower.

"No," – Sylvia tosses a sapling onto the wheelbarrow – "I'm still talking to you, Uncle Harry." But her back stays turned.

"Sylvia," Harry says, "be reasonable. Let's talk about this."

And when she still doesn't answer: "What are we going to do about this property?"

"*We?*" Sylvia rolls her eyes at Sandile. "What *we?* Since when do *you* own this land?"

"I own a bordering property," Harry says. "I have a say in what goes on here too, you know."

Sylvia knows better than to take the bait. Without pausing, she kneels to loosen the next Port Jackson.

"Let's talk about this like mature people," Harry says.

"You don't behave like a mature person," grunts Sylvia.

"Neither do you. What kind of woman uses language like that?'

"You drove me to it."

"I was upset. Sometimes you do these things and you just won't listen."

"*I* don't listen?" At last Sylvia stands to face him, curls gummed to her sweaty face. "*You* don't listen to *me*. You *never* listen to what other people have to say."

"Okay, okay." Harry's stick sails into the air behind him. He plants his feet side by side on the path. It's difficult to keep balanced but he does. Hands clasped at his back, mouth noosed in concentration, he stares at Sylvia.

"I'm listening. I'm listening to you now, Sylvia, and I'm not going to butt in."

Sandile jabs the pitchfork into the ground. Dig, pull, dig, pull. He's had a lifetime of learning not to interrupt, or even let on he's listening to Harry. Besides, he's heard it all before.

"Uncle Harry," Sylvia sighs, "I only want to do something about this place because it meant so much to my sister. I don't want to sell it. If I could, I'd keep it the way it is. But obviously I can't afford that. I had this really stupid idea …" With the palm of her hand she smacks dust from her jeans. "I don't know. That I might make some kind of – I don't know – *memorial* for Connie here. A bench with her name on it. Maybe. Something."

Harry stares at his feet, concentrating. While she waits, Sylvia's gaze wanders past him to Ivor and Janice at the back gate. Ivor has his hands in his pockets and Janice's arms are folded. They're a good distance apart but they're both watching Marianne lead Bart down the newly cleared path.

"Can I speak now?" Harry asks.

Sylvia looks back at him. She nods.

"Sylvia." Harry shakes his head. "This property's worth a lot of money."

"I know," Sylvia says. "Stupid idea."

"And if we *do* set something up here, who's going to pay?"

"I *told* you it's a stupid idea, Uncle Harry. Nobody's got the money to set up a park."

"Letty's got money. Her Auntie Miempie's just left her a bundle."

"You can't just take Letty's money!"

"Bullshit. She's an heiress now. Always giving money away. Orphans, holidays for pensioners, the Donkey Sanctuary. Give, give, give. Money burns a hole in her pocket. About time she put it into something worthwhile. Hey, Let?" Harry yells to where his wife stands at her kitchen door. "How's about we open up a park here for Connie West?"

"Uncle Harry," Sylvia says.

"We could put Letty in one of those khaki uniforms and she could hand out tickets at the gate!"

"I knew this would happen," Sylvia says.

"She could wear one of those game-ranger hats!" Harry

exclaims. "Listen," he tells her, "listen: we could plant more yellowwoods and start a *parrot* sanctuary. Have you ever thought of that, Sylvia? Hey? Hey?"

"Sis man, Harry," calls Alwyn from the bottom end of the plot.

"Actually, that's not a bad idea," Sylvia says. "We've all noticed there are a lot fewer parrots than there used to be. It might save you from climbing up a ladder with a pistol."

"It was a pellet gun," Harry says. "We'd get birders from all over the country. Letty could sew us staff uniforms in parrot colours: green, yellow—"

"I've had enough." Sylvia turns on her heel.

"The Letty Healey National Park!" Harry bawls after her. "The Letty and *Harry* Healey National Park! Alwyn can keep snakes on the side!" Then: "Okay! Okay!" He throws up his hands. "How about a compromise?"

He waits for Sylvia to turn around before continuing.

"Sylvia. Look." Harry's voice is serious now. "I'm not saying we can make this place a national monument or whatever you want to do. But I'm willing to support you if you want to try. I can get Letty to put money into maintaining the place. But *you*," – finger in Sylvia's face again – "must organise for netting over all my fruit trees. We'll raise funds. I'll get Toppie de Bruyn to kick things off. You can ask your friend the mayor over here for something, too."

"Are you serious now?" asks Sylvia.

"Serious." Harry raises his voice so everyone on the plot can hear. "I would do this for you. And for your sister."

"What about your pecan-nut trees?"

"I've told you. You can put netting over them. Letty can buy pecans from the Spar."

At this moment, Letty is opening her back gate to step onto the path. Even Princess has abandoned her washing to join the rest of them on the plot. Hands on hips, glaring at Harry, she plants herself just behind Sylvia. Princess is the only one who's never surprised at what Harry Healey gets up to.

"If I do this I want my name on the programme," Harry says, "and you have to promise to go to secretarial college in PE."

"I don't know …" Sylvia says.

"And you have to make tea once a day and come drink it with me. Also one of your milk tarts once a week. Alwyn!" Harry barks. He hasn't noticed Alwyn right behind him. "We're dedicating this place to Connie West. My idea. We're going to raise funds and have an indigenous garden and an education centre. Letty will pay. We'll have a dedication ceremony!" Harry flings an arm in the direction of his house. "Alwyn! Run fetch that bottle of Babycham I was saving for Letty's birthday, man! Oh no, can't send him, he's got a dicky heart. Sand—" Too late, Harry stops himself.

All this time he's been digging steadily with his back to the rest of them. But when he hears his name, Sandile turns slowly around. From behind the fogged-up lenses of his spectacles his eyes burn at Harry Healey.

"I'll go," Sylvia says, "I know where it is."

Before anyone can argue, she's off. Hair flying, breasts jolting, she thunders up the path towards Harry's back gate.

"If you can't find the Babycham," Harry yells after her, "bring a bottle of Coke instead!"

She was always his favourite. That was no secret. We all knew if we wanted something – a driver's licence, say, or permission to alter the house – Sylvia was the one to ask. All you had to do was get her to deliver a cup of tea when Harry was pottering in the workshop or the orchard. From a safe distance, behind a tree or in the shade of our back stoep, Alwyn and Ivor and I would watch Sylvia win Harry over for us.

She'd stand under the pecan tree, one leg rubbing the calf of the other, while Harry pursed his lips over the tea, or poured it in the saucer to cool. She always knew exactly the right moment to ask: *Uncle Harry, we were wondering if we could use the town hall next week for a disco?*

Jesus Christ. Can't a guy ever be off duty? That's how it always began. Couldn't a man drink a cup of bloody tea without someone coming to ask him for yet another thing? When were we going to learn to look after ourselves instead of always expecting other people to do it for us? He wasn't going to be there forever, you know. To sort out all our cock-ups. Etcetera. Etcetera.

Sylvia would scratch a pattern in the ground with her big toe, looking down as if she were a million miles away. Eventually, though, we all knew how it would end

Ja okay, alright, you can have it. Now bugger off.

Thanks, Uncle Harry.

Sylvia would step forward to hug him, and he'd pretend to fend her off. *Ja ja okay, now bugger off.* Shoving the cup and saucer back at her: *This tea's too weak. I like it strong.*

As Sylvia thuds up the dirt path towards Harry's back gate, she doesn't see that Sandile, too, has anchored his pitchfork in the soil next to the wheelbarrow and sprinted up the steps of the back stoep to pull his tee-shirt back on. Instead of following Sylvia, though, he's loping away from the others down the path towards the river. Everyone's too busy listening to Harry hold forth about parrots and plants to notice Sandile grabbing the rope at the wild peach and swinging himself to the other side.

Certainly Sylvia is too flushed with success to take in much else. She's pulled off what she'd been planning all along. Now it's just a matter of managing it. And everyone knows that will mean Harry wanting his share of the pie.

Chapter 31

IT'S DIFFICULT WHEN YOU'RE trying to put a picture across to somebody else. So many things happen at once. It's up to you to choose which details to include, how to arrange them so whoever's listening can join the dots for themselves. It's in your power to make another person see what you want them to see.

Of course, Dr Mkhaliphi's way too clever for that. He knows there's a big piece missing from the story I've almost finished telling him. And even though he's not on my back stoep any more, I've got a feeling he's somewhere around, listening. He may be up on the Kanonkop again. Or peering through Alwyn's kitchen window. Wherever he is, I know he's watching the rag-tag group of my family and friends trickle down the path towards the yellowwood tree. And that he's following my story right through to the end.

Too late now to pretend I don't want to be here. I do. I want – and don't want – to see how events play out. Can I change anything? Possibly. Gratitude, as Sylvia said, doesn't cost a thing. And if I'm here to tell the Boatman the story – if telling the truth is what it's all about – here is where a crucial piece fits in.

Right here under the yellowwood, where Ivor's squinting

up into the thick cloud of leaves, arms folded over his tight chest.

What's he doing here on his own, ahead of the others? Hasn't he heard what Alwyn just hoicked from the upper branches?

Go ahead, Ivor. I'm waiting. In my denim jeans, my sheepskin jacket and my hiking boots, just as I was the day before the wedding, my face tanned from the November sun, that haunted look in my eyes. Dog-tired because I'd been up since five a.m., not able to sleep. You could tell yourself you're imagining things. It's been a long day. It's hot. You're under stress. And that scene with Janice – well. But we both know why we're here.

This was all it took: an old dog pillow, a summer's night, a bottle of cheap wine.

When I got home that night my jersey sleeves were daggered with blackjacks. The buchu smell stayed with me for days.

Right here. Under the yellowwood tree was where it all began. Or was it?

The day before the wedding, the hammering and raised voices from Ivor's house drifted across to my place from early on. At my kitchen window I stood and watched two men in overalls pound in poles for a tarpaulin in the back yard of number fourteen Bloubessie Way.

I'd taken the day off. At first I lay in bed and tried reading for a bit. But I gave up after half an hour and shut all the windows and doors and got stuck into the house. Did two loads of laundry; made the bed; cleared out the spare room. I even cleaned Sylvia's room and changed her sheets for her. (I was pretty sure she hadn't slept in that bed for weeks.) Then I scrubbed the kitchen floor, though Princess had done it only the day before. I was itching to get into the garden, but I didn't want to be seen. That's when I tried picking up a book again.

Then, of course, Bart rang my doorbell and we had that argument. And after I'd phoned him back to say I'd go to the beach the next day, I went to the lounge and poured myself a G and T.

Naturally, I'd been invited to the wedding. Janice always believed in keeping things civilised. Etiquette demanded I be invited, and etiquette expected me to decline. I'd only hesitated five seconds before doing the right thing.

I ended up having three G and Ts that afternoon, and when I finally put the gin bottle back in the drinks cabinet, I found my way to my room and slept for three hours.

I woke at five o'clock. The shops were shut and the streets were deserted. People were either playing tennis or golf or having tea with each other. The hammering from Ivor's yard had stopped. A dry feeling in my mouth spread right down my throat and into my lungs and gut.

For about an hour I lay there, watching the shadow of the plum tree shiver on my bedroom wall. Then I got up and pulled on my hiking boots.

I climbed right to the top of the Kop that afternoon, even though I'd set out so late. It only started to get dark around seven, so I still had a good view when I got to the plateau under the red rock at the top.

I lay on my stomach beneath the rock and stared down at the valley below. In Ivor's back yard, the white tarpaulin was stretched out like a giant mushroom. There was just enough light for me to see people carrying out stacks of white plastic chairs, and Ivor at the back door, pointing and barking instructions.

I hadn't seen him in weeks, not even at a distance.

I watched the chairs being placed in rows facing the rose bower near the back gate, and the water feature being cleaned and the edges of the path trimmed. Then I stood up and dusted off my jeans to start the trek down before it got dark. Just in case, I'd brought a torch.

I took the shortcut down Harry's side alley to cross the plot to my back gate. I knew Harry and Letty would be in their front lounge watching TV, so they wouldn't see me slipping past.

As I opened Harry's back gate and stepped onto the plot, I heard a car door slam in Bloubessie Way. *Bye Baby.* Janice's voice floated across, crystal clear. *Love you.* Then the Ford engine gunned into life and faded down the road.

I already knew from Sylvia that Janice was sleeping over at her bridesmaid's house that night. She believed in doing things the traditional way, did Janice.

It was a still night. I stood on the path from Harry's house listening to the click of Ivor's front gate and the crunch of his footsteps up the stone-chip path. The front door of number fourteen Bloubessie Way shut and everything fell quiet again.

There was something so final about the slamming of doors, the clicking of locks. Some being shut in, others shut out. It made me feel I didn't want to go inside just then. I wanted to be somewhere where I was a part of things. Where there were no gates or bolts to keep me separate.

It was almost completely dark by then. Nobody would have seen me change direction from my back gate and head towards the bottom of the plot. I'd already switched the torch off but I knew my way round that place like the back of my hand and I wasn't afraid.

Even though it was almost officially summer, the air was still edged with coolness. Sylvia must have come home to check on me, and she'd lit a fire in the dining room. When I looked back to duck under a spiderweb I saw it flickering through the kitchen window. Jakkals barked once, then stopped. For once she'd rather flop next to the fire than come out with me.

When the yellowwood was still a sapling, I'd sawed off the lower branches to make a clearing at the base of the trunk. In time, the upper branches swept to the ground, making a furry cave where nobody could see you. There was an old, rotting cushion lying there, left from long ago, when I'd gone down to plant bulbs on the plot. I'd used it to pad my knees while I dug, but after that Jakkals slept on it while she waited for me.

I dusted the cushion off and folded it so I could sit on the dry side. It was seeded with dog hair and blackjacks, but I had thick denims on, so it didn't matter much. I closed my eyes and leaned back against the tree, hugging my knees.

Above me, a couple of parrots shifted and clicked, annoyed. They'd started to nest in the tree by then. I wondered how Janice planned to deal with that, and with the racket they were bound to make the next day. I envied the way parrots managed to sleep through the possibility of danger – even if it was with one eye open. How they didn't expect life to get better; they just lived. When they found the sweet fruits of yellowwood or pecan nut, they let the whole town know how excited they were.

I was so deep in thought I must have missed the squeak of the back gate of number fourteen. I only realised someone was coming when I heard twigs snapping and the rustle of branches being pushed aside.

Quite a few people knew the turns of the paths across the plot to my back gate or down to the river. But there was only one other person (apart from Alwyn and Sylvia) who knew the way it twisted from Ivor's back gate down here to the tree.

I hugged my knees tighter and kept still. I'm not sure what I was hoping. If I was hoping. The swishing footsteps drew nearer, then came to a halt. A branch whipped back, and the fresh, tart smell of buchu swirled in at me. A pair of narrow brown veldskoens was planted on the ground just outside the cave. As I stared down at them, one foot staggered to the side, and the other shifted quickly to steady it. Then the branches parted and Ivor's face peered in at me. For a few seconds he kept there, grinning. Then he stooped and crawled in.

"Knew you'd be here," he said, as if we'd spoken only an hour ago, not six months. He held a bottle of pinotage in one hand and a cigarette in the other, and when he leaned back against the tree, I could smell them both on his breath. He passed the bottle to me and I gulped a good swig.

It was pretty dark in there, but every now and then a few slivers of moonlight slipped through. I could feel Ivor staring at me and eventually I turned to meet his gaze. His cold blue eyes were half closed, and he leaned away from me like he wanted to take me all in. His hair had been trimmed around his forehead and ears so the white streak was even more pronounced, and his whole face was opened up, like a slate wiped clean. He looked so youthful, it reminded me of the night of Sylvia's standard-eight dance, when he'd worn Alwyn's tux. He didn't blink as I stared back.

"You all set for tomorrow?" I asked.

"All set," Ivor nodded solemnly.

"Looks like it's going to be quite a party."

"Looks like it." He exhaled, and for a moment his face was blurred by smoke. Then I watched him grind the stompie into the earth with his thumb. "Don't take it too hard, Con."

"What?" My head snapped up.

"What's happening. The wedding. Don't take it too badly. It's not personal."

"What makes you think I'm taking it badly?" Before I could stop myself I added: "Don't overrate yourself, Ivor."

"Okay," he said, "sorry. Just thought I'd explain."

"Explain?" I asked coldly. "Why would you suddenly want to explain things *now*?"

"I don't know. I suppose …" I could tell he was itching to light up another cigarette, but instead he eased the bottle of pinotage from my grasp. "I suppose I feel I owe you some kind of explanation, that's all."

A few blocks away a child's voice wailed, "I don't want to go to bed." Harry Healey's kitchen door clapped open and shut. "Letty? Letty! Where the hell are you?"

"She's scared, Con," Ivor said once he'd lowered the bottle again. It was three-quarters empty by then. "She might look strong to you, but she's vulnerable. You see how she is with the parrots and the garden. She needs someone to look after her."

"You're that person?" When I finally spoke, my voice seemed so thin I felt it might float away and disappear.

"Well – yes." Ivor sounded almost smug. "I hope so. She needs me. And I—"

"You like to be needed? Is that it?"

"Precisely," he said crisply. He hated bitterness.

I couldn't think how to respond. I knew if I finally started talking I'd never stop. And the time for that conversation seemed long gone. Maybe he felt the same. Like I said, Ivor and I didn't need to speak to communicate. So we stayed where we were, passing that bottle of pinotage back and forth until it was empty.

"I love you, Con."

If it hadn't been just the two of us there, I'd have looked around to see who'd spoken. He said it in such a low, matter-of-fact tone, so different from before. The words hung between us, refusing to disappear. I dropped my forehead to my knees and hugged them tighter. The moon was right out by then, and I could see the moulded dimples of the cushion, with Jakkals' long white hairs shining on it.

"From that night you showed me around here. When you made me swing over the river." Ivor drew his arm back to throw the empty bottle. I think he was hoping to get it through the foliage and down towards the river bank. But it spun up and got stuck on one of the branches of the yellowwood. He was never much good at sport.

I didn't say anything when he put his arms around me. When we lay back, he squeezed me so tight I almost choked. I didn't stop him and I didn't encourage him either. For a long time we just lay there staring up at the moon trickling through the needles and listening to the parrots shifting and a baboon barking from the Kop.

But of course in the end I put my arms around him, too. It's not like I ever had much choice.

The ground was cold and hard under my back, and the soil slid in under my fingernails. The roots of the yellowwood rode up against my spine and the moonlight shattered against his newly trimmed hair and his eyes glinting down at me. Yellowwood leaves came spinning over us, and in the branches overhead the parrots cavilled irritably. None of it mattered to them.

Chapter 32

"HAVEN'T I?" HARRY's voice floats down the path towards the tree, pleading. "Haven't I always looked after you girls?" When he blows his nose you can hear him right across the plot.

"The funny thing is," – Sylvia's just behind him – "it was probably there all along and we never knew."

"They won't bother you if you don't bother them," Alwyn says.

"Over here, Janice," Sylvia cries. She's tied a red dishcloth to one of the Port Jackson saplings and she's waving it in the air to call them all in. Tucked into the back pocket of her jeans is the bottle of Babycham.

"Over here," Sylvia calls to the others. "Under the tree. Oh." She sees Ivor. "How did you get here so fast?"

She turns to help Janice over a crumbling ant heap.

"I want *you* to turn the first sod," Sylvia tells her. She knows Janice is going to need some winning over still.

Behind them, Bart lifts Marianne from his shoulders before ducking under a branch.

"This tree," – Harry jerks a thumb at the yellowwood, not noticing how nervously Bart looks up at it – "is a *Podocarpus henkelii*. Natural habitat of the Cape parrot. They're an endangered species now." He stops to picture a schoolchild, hand raised: *Dr Healey, what kind of a flower is that?*

"*Dietes grandiflora*." Harry gestures at the river bank. "Propagated by bulbs. Grows on the Kanonkop. I brought them down here myself."

"Connie planted those bulbs," grumbles Alwyn.

"I put in those bobbejaantjies too." Harry waves at a clump of small purple flowers nearby.

"*I* helped Connie plant them there," Alwyn says.

"Does anyone know what's happened to Sandile?" Sylvia brandishes the bottle of Babycham.

"Gimme that." Harry snatches the bottle and shakes it with both hands.

One by one, people are swinging over to the plot from across the river. A crowd has begun to gather under the yellowwood. Ambition and Vusi are still hanging round the edges, staring suspiciously up at the tree.

"They forgot this." Janice bends to pick up a grubby cushion and a pinotage bottle, then drops them into one of the green plastic bags.

"Can we start now, please?" asks Sylvia. "Can anybody tell me where Sandile's gone?"

"And that," Harry says, "is a paintbrush lily. We're going to plant more in *that* river bank over there."

"I want to say something too," Alwyn raises his voice. "I hope you okes are going to allow me to redress this ceremony. Connie was like a sister to me."

"Sylvia, how long is this going to take? Ivor and I must go soon."

None of them hears the BMW gunning up the driveway of number twenty-two until the hooter toots loudly three times and a car door slams shut. Seconds later, the gate to the plot squeaks open and Sandile appears at the top of the path.

Even in the setting sun, his white suit dazzles, and his black shoes gleam as he strides down the path towards them. Though he hasn't had time to shower, and here and there the beautifully ironed shirt clings to his skin. His Ray-Bans are perched on his head and he squints at the group staring at him from under the tree. He can still make out the odd branch strewn across the path, and he manages to step gingerly over them as he approaches the crowd. Stopping to dust his trousers off, he glares defiantly at Sylvia.

You wouldn't think Scheepersdorp could stretch too far by way of a mayoral chain, but over the years Harry made sure it was a decent one. *A sign of office*, he lectured us more than once. *You got to get people to respect the authority invested in you. Show them who's boss.* Before every important function Harry would set Sandile up on the back stoep with a bottle of Brasso and some cleaning rags. Then he'd go to the safe and bring out the mayoral chain to be polished.

Sunlight sparkles on the copper and silver links resting on Sandile's chest. Sandile hasn't noticed that some of them are twisted, and that the gold coin in the centre is lying back to front. Still, it glimmers and sways on the white silk of his shirt for all to see. Sandile drops his Ray-Bans into place and clasps his hands behind his back to face them all. *Your serve.* Nobody has the nerve to look at Harry, though everyone's waiting to see what he'll do.

And give him his due: Harry never turned a challenge down. He knows he's expected to provide the unexpected. From the centre of the crowd he shoves Bart aside and steps forward to face Sandile. Harry clears his throat noisily. He plants his hands on his hips. For a few seconds he studies the ground at Sandile's feet, moving his gaze slowly up from the mirrored shoes to take in the suit, the chain, the obscured eyes and finally the top of the dreadlocked head. Then Harry stretches his powerful fingers forward. With surprising deftness, he untwists the mayoral chain until it hangs straight again. He pats it into place so roughly Sandile almost staggers backwards. Then Harry shoves the bottle of Babycham at him.

"Let's hope," Harry says, "you make a better mayor than you did a caddy. If you'd given me a five iron instead of a wedge," he raises his voice for those at the back to hear, "I'd have won the Border and District Championships in '79."

Before Sandile can reply, Sylvia grabs the Babycham and shakes it several times. She shoves it back at him. "I'd like to ask the mayor," Sylvia announces, "to declare this plot open."

Sandile stares dubiously down at the bottle in his hands.

"Go on!" Harry yells, "get on with it, man. It's almost time for the news on TVI!"

Sandile surveys them all: Bart with Marianne in his arms; Princess nodding her head; Alwyn still clutching his wretched Checkers bag; Esmé purse-lipped beside him. Sylvia's arms are folded across her grimy tee-shirt and her wide forehead is streaked with dirt. She's so anxious for Sandile to start she's almost mouthing the words at him. She nods her head encouragingly and a snared duwweltjie quivers on the fringe of her bushy hair.

Even though his head is bowed as if waiting for a prayer, Ivor's arm has crept around Janice, who seems prepared to ignore it for now. She stands so straight and tall and so perfectly still.

Harry scowls at the bottle of Babycham in Sandile's hands. He glances up to search for Letty, standing a few metres away, whose head is also bowed in the setting sun.

Above them all, the wind soughs through the yellowwood. A few needled leaves settle in the partings between Sandile's dreadlocks and on the sunglasses now perched once again on his head.

"Constance West," says Sandile at last, "was a woman who loved this place."

"Amen, siyabulela, amen," Princess says loudly, bowing her head.

"Nathi siyabulela," the crowd murmurs in response.

"She was a strong member of her community," Sandile continues, "and she looked after this piece of ground. She loved the land and she loved the plants and animals that come here. She would want this piece of land to be for all of them." He holds up the bottle of Babycham. "I am dedicating this place to her."

He takes so long fumbling with the cork that Harry's hands begin to twitch, but at last a puny pop scatters champagne foam, spraying over Sandile's shirt and trousers and the mayoral chain. Without skipping a beat, Sandile places a thumb over the frothing bottle neck and walks slowly around the tree, pouring as he walks.

"Amen, amen, amen," Princess starts to sing. One by one, the women from Sandile's party join in. Ambition unrolls a baritone and Vusi and Goodwill fall in.

I could never hear singing like this without wanting to be part of it, melting into the sound. Now is no different. It all fits together like the thunderstorm two hours ago: the beat of rain, the baritone of thunder, the high notes of sun sparkling when the clouds parted again. I look around for Dr Mkhaliphi. It feels important to tell him. But he is nowhere to be found. The crowd begins to sway as they sing. They start shuffling from foot to foot. Some of them break into applause.

Sylvia turns to Harry. "I'm sorry I swore at you," she says.

"Don't be sorry. I was an arsehole." And Harry totters towards her, arms wide.

Over his sagging shoulders, Sylvia tries to smile at Sandile. She hopes nobody else can see the way Harry's shoulders are shaking, the damp patch he is making on the shoulder of her dirty tee.

Chapter 33

It was Letty who called me to go and fetch Harry that day. The red bakkie had been parked at the graveyard across the river since five a.m., well before sunrise. All that time, Harry had been sitting in the cab. I almost felt sorry for him. I knew how difficult it was for him to keep still that long.

After Letty called, I went out to my back stoep to try and see Harry from across the plot. As the sun blurred up, the red bakkie emerged from the mist. It looked like it was swathed in candyfloss, or caught in a spittlebug's nest. But once the mist started thinning, I could make out Harry's figure hunched over the steering wheel. When he thought we might not see him properly, he got out and crouched over the front bonnet with his head in his hands.

It was two weeks after Ivor's wedding and I had my own problems to think about by then, though nobody else knew about that yet. The night before, I'd woken twice to rush to the bathroom to throw up. But after Letty called me, I drank some water and forced down a couple of Provitas. Then I pulled on my jacket and boots and went down to the plot.

By the time I'd swung over the river and taken the shortcut

across Papendorf's property to the graveyard, the sun was almost completely out and the dew was sparkling on the long grass.

As I walked up to the bakkie, Soapy lifted her head from the front seat of the cab. She was drooling, and even though she couldn't see me by then, her tail still thumped against the plastic upholstery of the seat.

I knew Harry had heard me coming, because when I got to the opened driver's door the rifle resting between his legs was cocked and ready, though it was pointed at the sky.

I pulled the rifle out of his hands. Then I put the safety catch back on. I knew the bullet chamber would be empty. How long had I known Harry Healey? Neither of us said a word.

I laid the rifle on the back of the bakkie and covered it with a mealie bag, then I stood aside for Harry to get out, and I climbed into the driver's seat. Harry could find his own way home.

For a few minutes I stroked Soapy's head until she fell asleep. Then I drove down the cemetery driveway, out of the iron gates, straight to Main Road and the vet's surgery.

And this is the point of what I'm telling you. This is what I find so strange: we are not necessarily kind to animals. We use them, we eat them. But we don't like them to suffer.

Yet humans must. They have to wait for the great Vet himself to decide how long their anguish must last and how deep it must reach. And He has, as far as I can see, a habit of waiting a long, long time before deciding to end their misery.

And you see the trouble is I never. Never. Could bear anyone else telling me what to do.

I let her do it finally, because I felt sorry for her. She only wanted to help. Maybe it was too much dagga, maybe it was too much being on my own, but I even began to believe there was a minuscule chance her prayers might work. Who knows?

Joko tea brewed three times and kept in a covered cloth in the kitchen's biggest pot. I had to drink it morning and evening. Then I had to stand in front of her with my naked scalp bowed while she lit a long taper of *The Scheepersdorp Herald* and circled me. While she scattered ashes over my skull, her warm breath muttered in my ear. It was strangely comforting.

By then I'd tried every lotion and potion known to man. Shiatsu, massage, buchu tea, kankerbossie and of course the dagga. Hope was a flame burned down to an ember, and they were all crouched around it, Sylvia and Sandile, Bart, Harry, Princess and Alwyn. And me. I didn't want to be the one to douse the fire, but I'd had enough. All those stages people told me about: anger, denial, bargaining, acceptance. In the end I just wanted peace.

I remembered Soapy, and the kindness we'd shown in easing her suffering. What was the point of waiting? Things weren't going to get better. That was the other reason I let Princess pray over me. I had a favour to ask. And of all the people I knew, she was the one most likely to help.

Chapter 34

ONE, TWO, THREE SCOOPS of earth. Everyone watches Alwyn jab the spade into the soil until he's deepened the six neat holes to the right level. Then he stoops to pick up the Checkers bag he's been carrying all afternoon.

"This is a memorial to my friend Connie," Alwyn announces loudly. "A tributary from me."

He shakes the packet out, dropping six pink bulbs into his palm, then folds his long legs in to kneel. One by one, he presses the bulbs into the soil. When he gets to the last hole, he slips in the Ziploc bag with its blue envelope from the garden shed and pats it down with his hands. In the last heat of the setting sun, he stands to reach for the spade again. But before he starts shovelling earth over the bulbs, he stops to wipe his forehead with the back of his sleeve. Sweat is blooming under his arms and in the small of his back. Alwyn parks the spade and fiddles with the buttons of his khaki shirt.

From the top of the path, Dr Mkhaliphi stumbles towards us at last, almost tripping over a buchu bush. He's back in suit and tie, but his head's still clean-shaven. As he walks, he loosens his tie and fingers his own striped, stained shirt.

For every button Alwyn undoes, the Boatman tries matching him. But he's too drunk to keep up.

"Look white boy!" Dr Mkhaliphi bellows at last, ripping the shirt open. "Look at the man who gave you this!"

The cavity in his hollowed chest glistens. The blood-soaked cave where his heart once nestled is a clue, a secret made flesh. Dr Mkhaliphi lifts a tiny index finger to his temple. He waits to catch my eye before pulling it like a trigger.

"Pow," he whispers, and slumps to his knees.

Almost six o'clock. The sun is dissolving into hot, messy globs of light between the aloes on the Kanonkop and the shards of buffalo grass on the plot. A white-eye launches from the plumbago hedge and a twig springs back, trembling. Within minutes, the leaves have melted into a purple scumble.

After all the excitement, Sandile's had to reverse his BMW down the driveway and park in Plumbago Way so the gardening bakkie can get out. The Bantam's loaded with bulging green bags and pointed towards the road. Spreadeagled over the bags, Ambition lies exhausted. Vusi and Goodwill perch silently on the sides, crammed between edge trimmer, buzz saw, rakes and spades, eager to get home. With the flat of his hand, Ambition beats on the roof of the cab three times. Shorty de Villiers shifts the bakkie into first and it rolls on down the drive.

"Bloody park, can you bloody believe it." Harry shuffles along the path towards his back gate. "Protected species. National bloody monument, my arse."

"Thank you, Uncle Harry." Trotting beside him, Sylvia reaches a hand out to steady him.

"Leave me, I can manage." Harry throws her off. "Nothing but trouble, you and that sister of yours. Not a day's peace since the day you were born."

On he stumbles, over dust and roots along the newly cleared path. But you can't toss *me* away, Harry. Not this time. I know you better than anyone. I know, for instance, why you're struggling so hard to pull air into your lungs, and about the pills and syrups and suppositories the chemist delivered this morning to clutter up your bedside table. I know about the block of stinkwood in your workshop, polished to a sheen and carefully stencilled, waiting for you to carve the words out with your routing machine: *Connie West: 1966–1994. She loved this place.*

I'm here at your shaking elbow as you fumble with the latch of your gate, shouting for Letty to put the kettle on. Just for you I've put on a skirt and a clean blouse. Maybe it's hard to recognise me with my hair combed so neatly. And for once making an effort to smile.

Not long now, I whisper in your ear.

Nobody sees you shoot me a grateful, glowering glance.

Perched on Bart's shoulders once more, Marianne crows. She throws up her arms and a giant shadow leaps on the path ahead. Behind them, Sandile trundles the wheelbarrow cautiously so as not to dirty his suit or mayoral chain. Sylvia is at his heels, pitchfork over her shoulder.

I loiter under the yellowwood, watching Princess climb the steps to the stoep, a plastic wash basket on her hip. Next door, Esmé and Alwyn, too, are mounting the stairs to their front door. At the top step, Alwyn drapes his arm round his mother's shoulders. He doesn't look back before going inside, and I can't help feeling a pang of regret. Lines from one of the dog-eared pages in Maggie's books flare up in me:

And they, since they / Were not the one dead, turned to their affairs.

Chapter 35

FROM LITERALLY THE DAY I brought Marianne home, Princess would spend afternoons on the plot with her. At first, she'd strap the child on her back with a blanket and walk down to the river, away from the house where she was disturbing me with her crying. As the days grew warmer, Princess would spread a blanket under one of the trees and let the baby kick in the sun for a bit. Whenever I got up to go to the bathroom or get myself something to drink, I'd stop to watch them through the kitchen window: Princess sitting on the blanket beside Marianne. They were usually somewhere near the yellowwood and the mound of earth where Princess once buried the baby's cord.

They'd sit there for up to an hour at a time, Princess picking plants, singing to Marianne, or rocking her until Sylvia went out on the stoep and called them in. Esmé kept trying to tell Sylvia she shouldn't allow Princess to take the child down there. She even tried getting me to interfere, but I made it clear I trusted my sister. And that I trusted Princess even more.

If anybody knew that place better than I did, it was her.

Now I can hear Princess's slippers shuffling up the steps of the back stoep. The floorboards creak and the kitchen door slaps shut behind her. And at last I remember. I remember everything.

In summer, the gazanias and bobbejaantjies blaze back at the sun. In winter, the rhus cling to their leaves but the wild peach sheds them, leaving itself naked and cold. And the alien jacarandas sing purple all down Plumbago Way.

Only humans don't die in the right season.

I died on a sunny day. At six a.m., the coolness of the night had started to evaporate. By nine, it was obvious it was going to be stinking hot. I noticed this briefly.

They brought Marianne in to say good morning to me. As usual, she wasn't keen. Her hair was gummed to her clammy forehead and she fretted in Princess's arms, refusing to be set down. Sylvia, too, ambled in. She'd been up all night, and she was still in the cotton shorts and tee-shirt she'd slept in.

"Con?" She perched on the edge of the bed. "Con, darling?"

Darling. I must have turned my eyes towards her because she started to cry. She shouted something and Princess came running with the portable phone. Sylvia grabbed it and left the room, while Princess stayed watching from the end of the bed. She had a yellow dishcloth in her hands, and she kept twisting it while she sang.

After that, there were no edges or borders any more. For weeks, I'd stared at my counterpane; at the edge of the bed just below the line of the window frame. And beyond the window frame, the horizon above the Kanonkop. This was the framework of my days. I knew all the sounds of the house, and I pieced them together to form pictures of what lay behind them.

That day was not that different: the rasp of Princess pulling the lounge curtains open; the knocking pipes that ached through the old walls when Bart or Sylvia showered. At lunchtime, the smell of umngqusho drifted down the passage, along with Princess's voice singing to Marianne. Then there was the palaver and crying of the child waking up again. After that everything dissolved and I heard only my breathing, like water lapping in and out of a cave.

At one point Bart came in. They'd called him home, though he'd been popping in all day. He held my hand and said something about looking after Marianne, about making me proud of her. He might have told me he loved me. Again.

The rest of them all wandered in and out: Esmé, Sandile, Letty.

Later, the screen door in the kitchen slammed open and shut again. I recognised the light, urgent tread hurrying up the passageway, even though it sounded heavier, a little more slurred than it used to be. The door opened and Harry fell to his knees beside my bed, dropping his face in his palms. There was the usual film of sawdust over his thinning curls, and I noticed a curled green parrot feather caught on the crown.

I heard him muttering into his cupped hands. I knew he wasn't asking for a miracle, or something that would make him out to be the hero who'd finally swung it so the miracle appeared. He was begging for mercy. It was the only kind of prayer I was happy to allow. I stared at his hands, one clasping mine, the other still supporting his head. I wondered when I'd stopped seeing him as so huge and terrifying. His fingers were square, as if they'd been cut from a template with a pair of sharp scissors. I'd noticed them before, of course, but always when they were busy sawing or hammering or pointing in my face.

I wanted to say. I wanted to say I was sorry for him. That he shouldn't take it too badly. That it wasn't as awful as he might think. But when I opened my eyes again he'd disappeared.

Gravity evaporated after that. Time sailed out through the

window, into the blue sky over the Kanonkop. And I dwindled in the middle of it. I wasn't pegged down to a paltry hour or minute any more. Shadows from the cupboard and the chairs softened and spread out and the air in the room glowed a softer, oily yellow. A fly buzzed at the window.

No more pain.

For three months the discomfort had been nesting inside me, flexing its muscles and tightening. Now it had finally moved on. Good. Let it bother someone else.

I noticed Ivor beside the bed. He tapped a pale finger at my drip and took my pulse.

"Con." His voice sounded strange. "It won't be long now, Con."

What I wanted to say was: remember the night I made you cross the plot? Remember how I said the snakes were more scared of you than you were of the snakes?

When I looked up again I tried smiling at him, then I saw it was Bart. Something I wanted to tell him. What?

"I just want it to be over," I said. My teeth were chattering. "I'm not scared."

Bart folded the blankets back and slid his arms under my back. Then he shifted me across the sheets and I heard the mattress squeak under the weight. I felt his heat and heaviness.

He took my face in his hands and kissed me.

"Me neither," he said.

When I opened my eyes later, Princess's face was hovering over me. From the far end of the room other voices echoed and faded. Marianne was calling. For once not crying but blurting happy, baby sounds as if they'd bubbled onto the tip of her tongue. I heard Sylvia murmuring in the passageway, then Bart. Princess turned, and Bart's thick fist closed quickly around the handle, pulling the door shut. His footsteps faded down the passage.

I heard a truck driving down Plumbago Way, grinding gears, and the distant wail of the train from PE approaching Scheepersdorp. Air trickled relentlessly into my lungs. I opened my eyes again.

For God's sake, Ivor.

But it was only Princess. She was singing under her breath. Eyes shut, she swayed from side to side, hands slack at her sides. Every now and then she did an almost imperceptible hop as she shifted from foot to foot. Over and over she wound the words out, shadowed and sticky, until I was wrapped in them, tight as a cocoon.

What she was singing: the same tune she's been singing all day.

I understand it again now, just as I understood it the very first time she sang it to me, a year ago today.

Ndiyakuncedisa ukugoduka uhambe kahle.

I am going to release your breath so that you can rest.

Princess's song picked me up and carried me down to the plot. It was a sweltering summer's day. The gazanias were unfolding over the baked earth. A drowsy fly was crumpled in a spider's web, swaying in the hypnotic heat. The spider's poison trickled down my bones and through my lungs, which struggled stubbornly to pull at the useless air.

Something cool and silky brushed across my mouth, my nose. Cotton. Feathers. Behind it, the weight of hot fingers.

Ikhaya lakho liyakubiza, ndizokukhulula umphefumlo wakho uphumle …

The singing swelled, *Your home is calling you*, louder and louder, until it nudged the air aside. The weight on my face pressed down more firmly.

No need. I wasn't going to resist. The dam was stopped up. The river had finally run dry.

The singing didn't stop, it just grew softer. A trickle ending in a quiet pool.

Down on the plot, on the bottom branches of the yellow-wood, a spiderweb swayed. To and fro like a hammock it swung in the hot wind from the Kanonkop, cradling its still and peaceful treasure.

Chapter 36

I KNOW WHERE TO FIND HER. I know she's waiting for me. Right here where she spent afternoons torturing me with that bloody radio, humming that annoying tune.

I'm not frightened any more. Of coming into the house. Of approaching her. Down the long passage I drift, past the wall photos and the bedrooms and the kitchen to the bottom of the house, where the laundry light's shining. There's a basket of clothes folded neatly next to the ironing board, and the smell of Skip and fabric softener has scrubbed the room clean.

Each time Princess leans down, the bangles on her wrists clink. Her fingers strain buttery yellow on the iron, and she hums as she steers it, a ship on a sea of white cotton.

For the first time today, I'm certain I am where I'm supposed to be.

Darkness has leaked into the room. In the breeze outside, a plum tree taps its leaves against the kitchen window, calling Princess to attention.

"Sjoe," – she parks the iron and wipes her forehead with a folded handkerchief – "kushushu namhlanje!" She flattens the shirt collar onto the ironing board with her palm. Then: "You must go back now," she sighs. "Is not time for you to stay here now, Connie." She sprays water onto the shirt collar and smiles at me from the corners of her eyes. And starts humming that tune again.

But it won't work on me. Not this time. I'm here to fit the last few pieces of the puzzle in for the Boatman. And for me. I know what I must do before half past six.

I sidle up beside her, close enough to stir a rash of goose pimples on her scrawny, berry-brown arms. I'm in Bart's blue-and-white-striped pyjamas, hopelessly too big, and my worn sheepskin slippers, with my hair just starting to grow back after I'd finally given up on everything.

You did it. For me.

Princess's eyes roll back to the whites. *Ndiza kukuncedisa uku-goduka*, she starts warbling, *I will help you go home.*

But *this* is home.

I should be grateful I've finally figured it out. Figuring it out means I get to go back. To move on, as they say. (How I hated that expression!) But when did any of us ever feel what we should?

"Is no good now, Con. Is time you must go back." Princess's head drops back and she starts to sway, her bony hips bumping the ironing board. "One day," she sing-songs, "we all going to come there. We going to come see you there when it's the time for us."

You won't come see me. You'll be too busy visiting those ancestors of yours.

"Oh Connie," her hoarse, phlegmy laugh, "we got lots of time there for the visiting. We not got the things like the apartheid there." Princess shakes her head. "Go back, Connie. We going to look after Marianne for you. She going to be the nice girl one day."

* * *

At the bottom of the driveway, Dr Mkhaliphi taps at the gold watch on his wrist. It's not an unkind gesture. He's looking more relaxed in an open-necked shirt and chinos, and his hair is lush and springy again. The sun has dropped halfway behind the Kop and street lights are beginning to flicker on. Dr Mkhaliphi holds both palms up at me, fingers spread: *ten minutes*.

There's very little left of me now. Only a last flash of light against a window, a squeal in a familiar tone as Princess takes Marianne from Bart for her supper time. In the bedroom that once belonged to Sylvia, the walls are bare and the cupboards emptied of their clothes. Two large suitcases and a laundry bag are parked at the door.

"Is that everything?" asks Sandile. He tests the weight of the suitcases and decides to leave the heavier one for Sylvia.

"It's enough for now." Sylvia still hasn't showered. In her sweaty gardening gear she's opening and slamming drawers as she rummages through her desk.

"What's this?" Sandile flips open a dog-eared book. "I didn't know you read poetry."

Sylvia glances up. "Where did you get that?" she asks. "It's one of Connie's books."

"It was here on your bedside table."

"Strange. I never put it there." Sylvia shrugs and goes back to searching the desk, setting aside a roll of sticky tape.

"'I heard a Fly buzz – when I died'," Sandile reads. "Hey, this isn't bad. Listen here, Syl: 'Success is counted sweetest / By those who ne'er succeed.' We should show it to Harry."

"Baby. Give it a break." At last Sylvia has found what she's looking for. She bends over her old desk with a book opened in front of her. Flipping expertly through, she finds the page she wants and spreads it open with her palms. Then she snaps off a piece of sticky tape and presses a lock of hair onto the page, her tongue curling out from between her lips.

My First Haircut, says the title at the top. And in her beautiful, plump cursive Sylvia writes the date: *4th November 1995.*

Across the passage, in my old bedroom, Bart slumps on the unmade bed, broad back rounded to read the sheet of blue notepaper in his hands.

It's strange, again, to examine the marks my human hands once made. As if he's thinking the same thing, Bart strokes the first few letters with a chubby thumb.

Dearest Bart

See? You <u>are</u> dear to me. Here's proof in black and white.

Sylvia's got the papers where I've written what I want you to do with my jewellery etc. Please remind her I want the tiger's-eye pendant and the silver bracelets to go to Princess. All the rest is for Sylvia and Marianne.

I'd like you to keep all my books for Marianne until she's old enough to decide if she'll enjoy them or not. Also my bicycle.

Please read to her as much as you can.

I wanted to tell you that Scheepersdorp people love skindering. Screw them. If you ignore them long enough they'll find someone else to talk about.

I didn't choose to fall pregnant, but if I had to go back, I'd choose <u>you</u> every time to be the father of my child. I mean that.

I know this whole mess is my fault. Believe me: I didn't hold off on treatment because of you. That's the truth. Whatever else I may be, I'm no martyr. Please don't blame yourself. That would be unfair. And a waste of time.

Don't be too soft with Marianne. Don't be afraid to put your foot down with her.

Thanks for always treating me like <u>me</u>, not someone who was dying.

If things had worked out differently.
You would have been the much better part of me.
With love. Genuine.
Connie
PS Don't forget to get Marianne tested for allergies. She might be
allergic to penicillin, like me.

What he never knew I liked so much was how he'd dance with me, even on the worst days. When I put music on the hi-fi, he'd grab my hands and fling me out and in and out again like I was strong, not weak. He'd tuck his arm around me and twist and two-step me around the living room like I was a hard-hearted, tough old tart in a red dress with fishnet stockings and stilettos. Not a scrawny woman with no hair in pyjamas and slippers. Not like I was a piece of china that might crack any minute, but a real, live, flesh-and-blood being who could dish it out and who could certainly take it.

And I still can't say there weren't times I was happy. Times *we* were happy. Moments when everything seemed just right. I know that sounds strange when you think of the situation I was in, but there's also a freedom, as the song says, in having nothing left to lose.

Sometimes we'd be driving home, Bart at the wheel, me in the passenger seat, and that feeling would sweep in from nowhere. For a split second the world would seem cheerful. Not just cheerful: enchanting. The lampposts gliding past, the rich blue-grey of the asphalt, sun spanking off the rooftops, a woman skipping down the front steps of a house to welcome someone opening her gate. For that brief flash of time, everything seemed just as it was meant to be.

There's a dried-out ficus in a copper bowl standing on a trivet in the corner of the room. A weak shaft of light is lingering on the shrivelled leaves and the dust motes filtering down in the dusk.

Just a second or two of me in my green dress, the one I wore to the museum disco that night. I've still got the white sandals on, but any moment now I'll whip them off to dance with him, 'cause as I told him at the time: they're bloody killing me.

I never actually lied, is what I want to tell him, *I never told you everything but I never actually lied. I did what I thought best. Not just for me or her. For you, too.*

Marianne is calling from the high chair in the kitchen, where Princess is trying to feed her supper. Just for the moment, Bart ignores her.

He'll be there when she cuts her first teeth and on her first day of school. When she has her tonsils out he'll lumber down the corridors of Scheepersdorp Hospital dripping blobs of twirly-whirly ice cream. He'll sit on the stoep and sweat when a pimply boy comes to fetch her for her matric dance. In twenty years' time, he'll sit on the front stoep with a crate of beers, waiting for her to complete her twelve-hour trip home from university in Cape Town. And he'll never – even if he knows he ought to, even if he knows everyone else in Scheepersdorp is doing it for him – ever consider the possibility of Marianne being anything other than his own flesh and blood. His daughter. Because that's the kind of man Bart is.

As if he knows he has only seconds, Bart's studying me carefully. He straightens his face, mirroring mine. What a ridiculous expression! I tip my head to hide my laughter.

"I knew you couldn't keep that up for long," Bart smiles. He stares at the dust filtering through the dusk. At the glossy purple of the ficus leaves.

"That's okay, Con," he sighs at last. "I forgave you long ago."

One last call to make. Down the deep-red walls, the freshly painted corridors of the future I sweep, casting no shadow. The candy-striped curtains of the bedroom are now firmly closed. Ivor's shadow ruffles across them as he lifts his arms. He peels off his shirt and for once, instead of folding it neatly onto the chair beside the bed, he lets it slither from his skin. The metallic snap of his belt. He steps out of his trousers, still seeded with blackjacks from the plot. Onto the floor they slump, emptied of him.

Almost impossible to tell her head on the pillow from the shadows around her. Her eyes glitter as she turns her face away from him.

"Janice." He sits on the bed beside her, naked as a worm. He takes her hand. "I love you."

"Do you?"

Instead of answering, he pulls down the sheets to reveal the twin tendernesses of her breasts. The small dark shrub on its precious mound of pink.

Are they really made for each other? Perhaps not.

Neither of them has any thought of me. Nor of the rhus pattering against the glass of the French door or the yellowwood swaying fifty metres away. They don't hear the distant clang of the church bells, or Jakkals' nervous bark as she patrols the back fence. Or Sandile calling bossily to Sylvia as he lugs her suitcase down the front steps of number twenty-two to the BMW parked in Plumbago Way. They don't even catch the ear-splitting blast as he puffs up his cheeks and bites his gap teeth over his lip. They're certainly not aware of the Boatman cupping his hands to his mouth and calling my name. *Connie. Constance West.*

Janice sighs. Already she can hear the shriek of undisciplined children (not hers), the loud talk of picnickers next door. There will be very strict rules, she decides, finally unfolding her arms to her husband. They will put up a security hut and hire a guard. She lifts his hand and guides it across the pleasing planes of her hips.

"Janice," he groans, "darling. Oh, God."

"I love you," Janice gasps. Her fingers dig into his shoulders, and I float away. Lighter, freer, the giver of benign gifts. Far enough to look down at them; their flawed sweat, their twisted meanings. If they only knew.

Be careful what you ask for.

Already the seed is sinking into fertile ground. Already the captor is surrounding the captivated.

"And I said yea it shall be done and it was done," Dr Mkhaliphi mutters, pacing up and down the pavement outside my house. "Not a sparrow falls without Him knowing. Do not cast your pearls before swine, or your seed on fallow ground."

The wind whirls up. The sun drops like a stone. Right on cue the Kanonkop hunches back into place. Wishes are granted, dreams will come true. Ivor and Janice: this one's for you. Roses and warm blood don't last, but you wanted them anyway and here they are. For you. From me. Connie.

With love. Always.

Chapter 37

DR MKHALIPHI LIFTS THE oars in his small, spidery hands. The lake is flat beneath the darkness again, and the boat barely marks its surface, just two silver lines swerving in the water behind us. The gulp of oars dipping in and out.

I can make out very little now. The outlines of the Kanonkop dissolved long ago and the lights of Scheepersdorp lie in the distance like ground-up glass.

"And so you found it?" Dr Mkhaliphi asks. "You found what you were looking for?"

I nod. There's something I want to ask him, but I don't know how to start. I'm too familiar, by now, with the way his eyes flatten and his lids droop when he feels I'm being over-curious.

With each pull of his arms the Scheepersdorp horizon drags itself further away. We're halfway across the lake before Dr Mkhaliphi finally speaks again: "I'm not certain," he says, "that you would understand."

He stops, resting the oars. He folds his hands in his lap.

"God," he says suddenly, "is a comedian playing to an audience too afraid to laugh." For a second his miniature fingers flare up, then grow still. "What if you find yourself in a room full of people? And you look around you and everyone is laughing? Everyone except you?" He's staring past my shoulder towards Scheepersdorp, but his eyes suddenly focus on mine. "I did not want for food, I did not want for love. I had a good job. I had respect. I had a family and money." He shrugs. "But I didn't get the joke. I wanted to stop feeling that way."

Then Dr Mkhaliphi stretches out his palm. "Give it to me, please," he says.

I try to look puzzled, to find the same stonewalling coldness he's used with me for most of today. I'm not sure I pull it off, but at least I manage to meet his gaze without flinching.

"Constance." He shakes his head. "Connie. It's no good. If you don't leave these things behind, you cannot go back again."

"Don't want to go back," I say at last.

"Wena," he almost smiles, "you must listen to your elders now. One day, Constance, the child will come here herself. She may be an old woman by then. Let us hope so." His strange eyes gleam at me through the mist. "Maybe she will still be young. But you: you will know her straight away. You will be waiting for her. Over there you will be waiting." He tilts his head at the darkness behind him.

"I will take you there myself, Connie. I promise you."

"You are heartless," I say. But I lift my fist from my lap and uncurl it finally.

They're the colour of straw, or buffalo grass bleached by the sun. The strands are clumped together, still matted with sweat. One of them has a streak of green Smartie dye.

"You are a good mother, Ms West," Dr Mkhaliphi says. He leans forward to pinch the lock of hair.

"It is like you are running down a corridor of glass," – his voice is so low I can barely hear it – "and they are on the other side, carrying on with their lives. They can't see your face against the glass, watching them. Watching her. Yes, your name will trickle away. The days and weeks will go by. Years. Eventually there will be no mention of you, except on birthdays, at Christmas. She will forget. They will all forget. But you own a part of her nobody else does. And sometimes – when she frowns or she dances, or maybe she laughs at something you would have found funny, too – then, Connie West, you will rise in her face like a full moon over the Kanonkop."

Dr Mkhaliphi looks down at his hand for a moment, then eases it towards the side of the boat. I'm grateful for the gentle way he angles his palm over the edge.

The lock of hair makes only a small dent in the water. And as it floats down into the darkness, Dr Mkhaliphi looks up to catch my gaze. For the first time he smiles.

It's not like the sun coming out. It's more like a flash of lightning in a midnight storm. For those few dazzling seconds, the landscape ignites and everything is clear and comprehensible: the lake, the murky sky, the last pinpricks of light from Scheepersdorp. Even the darkness crawling towards us from the nearby shore.

I remember how it felt to be alive. How some nights I'd listen to my heart beat till it scared me, and I had to shift onto my right side to get to sleep. I remember how long the sheets would stay warm from the body beside me, long after it had left the bed. How my eyes would sting when I was tired, or when I stared too long at the Kanonkop on a summer's afternoon. And how, when I waded into the river, the water would push against my body as I entered it, like walking into a story.

The sounds of Scheepersdorp are dwindling away, but I know a child is being sung to sleep there, and that a man and woman are curled together in bed, spent. A light is on in a workshop where trembling hands are guiding a routing machine. In a house across the river, curtains are being drawn, suitcases unpacked. A dog-eared book of poems has been dropped onto a bedside table.

I know a bakkie with a hessian bag on the back is driving in the dark towards the dirt road on the far side of the Kanonkop. I can almost see for myself the lanky figure stooped to unknot that bag, the slow, green glide emerging to part the grass and head for the depleted forest of yellowwoods. The sudden panicked cacophony of parrots.

The Boatman can see this all, too. His sloe eyes are larger than the moon. They see everything. They contain everything. I want to lean forward and brush my fingertips against the skin of his hand, but already the edges are starting to dissolve. As if he's reading my thoughts, the Boatman nods at me.

Then he takes up the oars again. He leans forward and starts to row.

Acknowledgements

THE EMILY DICKINSON POEM to which Connie refers on page 120 is "We grow accustomed to the Dark" (*Unpublished Poems of Emily Dickinson*, ed. Martha Dickinson Bianchi & Alfred Leete Hampson, Little, Brown, and Company, Boston, 1935).

The lines of poetry Connie remembers on page 221 ("And they, since they / Were not the one dead …") are from Robert Frost's "Out, Out" (*Mountain Interval*, Henry Holt and Company, New York, 1916, p. 50).

The lines Sandile reads out on page 230 are from the Emily Dickinson poems "I heard a Fly buzz – When I died –" (*Poems by Emily Dickinson: Third Series*, ed. Mabel Loomis Todd, Roberts Brothers, Boston, 1896) and "Success is Counted Sweetest" (*Poems by Emily Dickinson*, ed. T. W. Higginson & Mabel Loomis Todd, Roberts Brothers, Boston, 1896).

In Dr Mkhaliphi's speech on page 236, he refers to a quote from H. L. Mencken: "CREATOR. A comedian whose audience is afraid to laugh" (*A Book of Burlesques*, 1916, Alfred A. Knopf, p. 203).